SECRETS OF Meynch

BOOK ONE OF ADVENTURES IN MEYNCH

Bezi Yohannes

Secrets of Meynch

Book One of Adventures in Meynch

Tate Publishing and Enterprises, LLC

Published by Tate Publishing & Enterprises, LLC
127 E. Trade Center Terrace | Mustang, Oklahoma 73064 USA
1.888.361.9473 | www.tatepublishing.com

Tate Publishing is committed to excellence in the publishing industry. The company reflects the philosophy established by the founders, based on Psalm 68:11,
"The Lord gave the word and great was the company of those who published it."

Cover design by Lauro Talibong
Interior design by Joana Quilantang

Published in the United States of America

ISBN: 978-1-62147-252-0
1.Fiction / Christian / Fantasy
2.Fiction / Coming of Age
12.09.20

DEDICATION

To Mom and Dad,
There's no way I could have gotten here without you.

Acknowledgments

To Mom and Dad for supporting my dream even when it was inconvenient to you. Thank you for your love and encouragement and for all the times you indulged my *slightly* obsessive reading habits.

To my favorite and only sister, Sophie, whose eternal optimism and adorable curiosity make my life interesting. I love you, sis.

To my extended family for your generous support and encouragement. A special thanks to Grandma and Grandpa for reading the first nine chapters of my story and giving me positive feedback at a time when I thought that I was a failure as a writer because I had hit my first writer's block.

To Kari S., thank you for taking the time to read my manuscript in its early stages and giving me constructive criticism as well as for being a wonderful small group leader for…ahem…energetic high school girls.

To the Soup, Delania, Jessica, Caitlyn V., and Christy, who agree that normal is so overrated. You showed me that I didn't have to have it all together because true friends accept you with your quirks, not in spite of them. This story would never have been born without you. Don't ever change.

To Sarah S., close friend and fellow fantasy bookworm. The greatest honor you could give would be to find this book a place on your bookshelf in Germany right next to *Hunger Games* and *Harry Potter*.

To all of my FBTA friends that I specifically promised I would mention in my book if it ever got published: Adriana and Veronica, other fellow fantasy bookworms; Gabby and Vanessa; Catherine M., my journalism mentor; Hannah Z.; and Keila and David B., my fellow debaters. And a shout-out to all my other friends at FBTA and my new friends in Hayfield that I don't have room to mention!

To Mr. Beard, because your recommendations and editorial counsel were invaluable in making this book the best it could be.

To Mrs. Mills, for calling me to walk out on faith. Thank you for telling me to look in the mirror and see with the eyes of Christ beyond the statistics that said I would never make it big as an author.

But most importantly, to Jesus Christ, the King above all kings. I have trusted in my own strength to stay close to You, and when I predictably failed to do what I knew was right, You still covered me in Your mercy and allowed me to approach You unafraid. I have been ashamed to call You my King, yet in love You still provided for me the desires of my heart. You guide me to do things I never dreamed I could do.

DAYDREAMING

"Abi?"

A young boy ran through the twisted corridors of a huge citadel. He murmured a hurried, "Pardon me," after colliding several times with lords and ladies, but he could not pause to apologize further. His mission was too important.

"Abi?"

He had to find the Council of Knights and tell them of the grave danger that lurked within the castle walls, the betrayal festering and spreading like the peasants' Black Plague. He ran faster, bursting into a large room—the council chamber. The golden-haired, majestic King Arthur sat at the head of his champions, the Knights of the Round Table, with his enigmatic mage Merlin standing behind him as they discussed the affairs of Camelot.

"Sirs?" the boy interrupted, breathless not only from his exertion but also from a sudden feeling of insignificance as he stood before such legendary men.

All heads turned to face him…

There was a loud cough. Abi Candial snapped back to the twenty-first century and into the uncomfortably warm classroom. Too late, she realized that the cough had been a signal, and she was about to miss something important in class. Like the teacher calling on her.

"Abi Candial, pay attention or you will be seeing me in detention!"

And there it is. Abi slowly lifted her head to see her English teacher glaring at her. "It's your turn to read," the stern-faced teacher said.

Abi stared blankly at the book in front of her. *Shoot. I have no idea where we are. This probably wasn't the best time to revisit imagine the glory of the medieval age…*

She looked around the classroom, focusing on the dark-haired girl sitting nearby. She tried to make eye contact and mouthed, *Where are we?*

Sarah glanced at Ms. Anderson and said, "Page twenty-four, second paragraph," covering her words with loud, hacking coughs. Abi smiled at Sarah's enthusiasm, but quickly hid her grin when Ms. Anderson's gaze swung back to her.

"Are you finished?" Mrs. Anderson tapped the dry-erase marker against her palm, her expression far from amused.

"Sorry, Ms. Anderson." Sarah instantly stopped coughing and tried to look wide-eyed and innocent.

"Abi, now that Sarah has conveniently recovered from her asthma attack, would you please honor the class by reading where we left off?" her teacher asked Abi impatiently.

Abi made sure Sarah caught her grateful smile before beginning to read.

After class, Abi threw open her locker and sighed. "That was a close call."

Sarah opened her locker more gently and stared at her reproachfully. "I'll say. Abi, you have got to wake up from your la-la land and pay attention in class, or you're going to get in a lot of trouble. I'm not always going to be there to bail you out." She flipped her long hair off her shoulder, a move only she could do and look elegant instead of shallow.

Abi turned to face Sarah and rolled her eyes. "Mrs. Anderson is just mean. Most of the other teachers don't care if I daydream as long as I get decent grades and don't act up."

"Oh, yeah, so when Mr. Smith caught you doodling the Colosseum in your math notebook, his class lecture that lasted for ten minutes straight on not wasting our education *totally* counts as not caring." Sarah paused. "Actually, now that I think about it, compared to other teachers, Mrs. Anderson is the nicest. She didn't even call me out on my 'asthma attack,' or make me go to the clinic like Ms. Lucas. Now *that* was embarrassing. I've covered your tracks so many times, but this isn't going to work anymore. My throat is getting scratchy from all the coughing. You need to come back to earth and stay here."

As much as Abi wanted to contradict her friend, Sarah was always right, at least when it came to the trouble Abi's zoning out caused. Though Abi was a good student and never in any real trouble, she was known throughout the student body and most of the faculty for her short attention span, which, of course, was not the best reputation to have if she wanted to be popular or buddy up to teachers.

"You're right, you're right. But that's nothing new. I'll figure out something. Anyway, at least that was last period. It's finally Friday! Doesn't that cheer you up? A whole weekend of relaxation!"

Sarah simply tilted her head and stared at Abi steadily.

"Come on, don't make me sing the song! I know how much you hate Rebecca Black." Abi grinned at Sarah, who finally smiled back, the seriousness disappearing.

"I don't know about you, but I'm going to be working this weekend. Our science lab is due on Monday, remember?"

Abi groaned. "Oh darn. I forgot. I have to call Marcus. He's an arrogant jerk and a horrible partner, but I'm stuck with him thanks to Ms. Lucas."

As Abi turned back to her locker to get her books and homework for the weekend, she glanced at her locker mirror and saw the reflection of a familiar face behind her. Without turning, she addressed him coolly. "Chris. We just described you in two words. Or at least your kind. The words 'arrogant' and 'jerk' ring a bell?"

"Hey, little sis. Great to see you too." Her dark-haired, lean older brother tossed her his signature dimpled, impish grin that girls had told her "makes him look a little like a younger Johnny Depp." *Gag-worthy.*

"I heard about your latest misadventure," he continued. "Tsk, tsk. Will you ever even try to pay attention in class? I heard Milton and Jed talking about you, and let me just say, you know you're a failure when even the nerds think you're weird."

Abi turned around slowly. "Oh? Now you're trying to spy on me? *That's* not creepy at all. So who told you?"

Chris ignored her and turned to Sarah. "I'm surprised she's even gotten to the tenth grade. I mean, she doesn't even bother to try and listen to the teachers."

"Yeah, right." Abi retorted. "You shouldn't even be talking, Chris. You need to grow up. You have what they call 'Perpetual Peter-Pan Syndrome.'"

Chris blew on his nails and rubbed them on his shirt. "Yep, that's me. Eternally young and handsome. Forever seventeen." He winked at Sarah, who stayed quiet, her eyes laughing. She had heard this argument many times before.

"More like eternally childish and immature. You're such a walking stereotype: the jock, the player, the annoying older brother. You couldn't be responsible if your life depended on it. And don't think you're going to distract me. Who ratted me out?"

Chris tilted his gaze towards Abi, seemingly nonchalant. "What were you saying? Oh, how did I know you were daydreaming again?" He shrugged. "I have my ways…" He raised his eyebrows at her furious glare. "You know, I never noticed this before, but you look really ugly when you get mad. I mean, some girls look cute when they're mad, but not you. Your forehead gets all wrinkled, and your eyes squint—"

"Chris! Shut up! You're so loud!" Abi noticed a cute guy walk quickly away with a smirk and realized he probably heard the entire conversation. *Ugh. Just my luck.*

She watched him out of the corner of her eye and noticed him stop to wrap his arms around a pretty blonde girl in a cheerleading uniform who had her back to Abi. *Of course*, she thought. *Why am I not surprised?* She fingered her own shoulder-length nondescript brown hair as she looked at the girl's blonde curls that fell perfectly halfway down her back.

The cheerleader and the boy looked straight at Abi, then laughed. Abi didn't need to hear their conversation to know what they were saying.

She is so weird.

I know, right? She doesn't even try to pay attention in class. And she's not even ADHD, so it's not like she has an excuse.

She definitely lives in la-la land. Does she even know what the real world is?

I doubt she even gets her head out of the clouds long enough to have a life.

Abi turned away and looked down at her shoes. She firmed her jaw. She wouldn't give them the satisfaction of seeing her hurt. *Yes, I know I'm weird, at least to you. But daydreaming isn't a crime, and la-la land is definitely more exciting than people like you and everything else I've got here.*

Looking up at her brother, she saw a flash of sympathy in his eyes, but it was so quick she almost didn't believe she had seen it. She hated that her feelings were so obvious. She glared at him. "Thanks for embarrassing me. Again. I bet you did that on purpose too."

Chris shrugged as if to say, *what do I care what you think of me?* "Since I know you're just dying to know, Tanya was the one who told me."

Abi and Sarah rolled their eyes knowingly. They both knew that Tanya would do anything to get attention, especially if it meant flirting with Chris. She had been after him since the seventh grade, and she didn't bother to be subtle about it.

"Wow, Chris, this is a new low, even for you," Abi said. "You actually believe something that comes out of the mouth of that—"

"Abi," Sarah said warningly.

Chris shrugged and said, "Hey, a guy's gotta do what a guy's gotta do. Getting the intel was worth the few compliments I had to give her."

Abi was about to reply, but at that moment, the dismissal bell rang. "Gotta run!" Chris winked at them and sauntered away.

Abi rolled her eyes again. She knew exactly what he was thinking. If Mom and Dad asked about how the day went, which they would, just like they always did, Chris would gladly tell them all about Abi's inattention, and probably exaggerate it to make them think it was worse than it really was.

Great. Now I'm going to get The Lecture. Thanks, Chris. Thanks a lot. As if my day didn't suck already, you just have to make it worse.

As she turned away, she noticed that Sarah's eyes were a bit dreamy as she watched him leave. "Sarah! You better not be thinking what I think you're thinking!"

"What?" Sarah finally looked at Abi.

"Please don't tell me that you have a crush on my brother!"

Sarah blushed. "Maybe. He's cute."

Abi stuck her finger down her throat. "Okay, first, eew! Second, have you not noticed the whole ego-the-size-of-Texas-and-maturity-the-size-of-a-pea thing he has going on? You can do better. Heck, any girl with some level of intelligence can do better!"

"Yeah. You're right." But Sarah's voice wasn't very convincing.

Seeing the bus pull up outside, Abi zipped up her backpack, tossing it over her shoulder. "This discussion is not over. I'm going to help you get over this. Are you taking the bus today?"

"Nope. Mom is picking me up. And Abi, relax. I just made an observation. You're acting like you're gonna help me through an drug addiction or something."

"No, this is worse than drugs."

"Really, Abi? Overreacting much?"

"Kidding! Just kidding. But really, you can do better." Abi tapped her chin. "With your looks, I can imagine you with a tall, dark, and handsome Italian."

"You better not be doing any more imagining. I told you, I won't risk bronchitis for you any more."

"I know, I know. Hey, wait a second, you're not taking the bus? I'm gonna have to suffer through the bus ride all alone?"

Sarah shrugged and picked up her bag. "Sorry. But you'll live, don't worry. Good luck with your parents."

Abi sighed. "Thanks. I'll need it."

After school, Abi decided to do some of her homework on the bus to distract herself from the chaos. She slid into an empty seat, put her backpack next to her so no one could sit beside her, and took out her books. But some jerk kept pulling her hair, and she couldn't focus on her work. When she finally turned around, the chubby, auburn-haired middle schooler attempted to look innocent.

With difficulty, Abi refrained herself from giving him a piece of her mind and leaned back against the seat. Her anger wasn't all his fault; all her nervous energy just needed an outlet. She knew exactly how her parents would greet her the moment she stepped through the door. She knew The Lecture so well, she could almost recite it word for word.

Abi's Punishment

"Abigale Michelle Candial, how many times have I told you that daydreaming is going to get you in trouble? And again and again, I have been proven right. If you ever want to succeed in life, you need to learn to come out of your la-la land and into the real world. You can't leave the planet when you're supposed to be doing school work."

Abi sat in her kitchen, staring at the tablecloth while her mother lectured her about "the evils of daydreaming."

Her daydreams were so much more sophisticated that just "la-la land." She envisioned worlds and characters in her mind, with such clarity that she felt she was actually there.

Abi wished that she could put into words the happiness she felt when she created a world of her own, a place where she could be in the midst of fierce battles, see magnificient kingdoms in all their glory, and live in the intrigue and mystery of a royal court without ever leaving her seat.

It was cheaper than going to a movie and better than TV or reading. In all those things, someone else shaped the story for her. But in her mind, she controlled the people, the places, and the events. The characters in her mind did whatever she wanted them to do, and she made them do pretty much everything. That feeling of complete and total power was intoxicating.

But Abi couldn't tell her mom all of that. She knew that the older woman would not, could not, understand. Abi could only sit and listen, wishing she was somewhere else.

A young officer sat with his comrades-at-arms as they eagerly ate their meager meal. They had not eaten in a long while, since before their ordeal at Valley Forge, and, though he could not speak for his compatriots, he was definitely most grateful for every scrap he received.

After they finished, the soldiers lounged around, talking and laughing over shared mugs of ale. The young officer was carrying on a lively conversation with the man beside him about their wives back home when a boy ran up to him and whispered something in his ear. He grimaced then dismissed the boy, giving him a gold coin. He turned back to the assembly of high-ranking officers. He hated to interrupt, being a relatively inexperienced officer compared to these men, who had been fighting since the French and Indian War years ago, and he was not high up on the chain of command. But this news was just too important to wait.

"Sirs?"He stood up to address the gathering. "I have just been informed that the British are planning to attack Yorktown."

General Washington paused in his hearty conversation with his commanders and stared at him. He tried not to flinch under the general's sure, steady gaze.

Then the general stood slowly. "This is grevious news, indeed. Yorktown is very near to where we are stationed now. Are you sure of this information?"

The young man gulped and looked around the campfire. The men all stared at him, making him feel like his answer would determine the course of the War for Independence. He closed his eyes and breathed a silent prayer then knew, without a shadow of a doubt, what his answer should be…

❧ ❧ ❧ ❧

"…so I am going to take away all privileges until you get your act together."

"Huh? What?" Abi blinked and looked up at her mom. Chris stood just behind her mom's shoulder, smirking, while her mom stared intently down at her.

"For the next week, the minute you get home from school every day, you are officially grounded. That means I expect you to do nothing but homework, like that science project with Marcus that Chris told me is due on Monday."

Abi shot Chris the dirtiest look she could muster. *Great. Just great. Could this get any worse?*

"Oh, and that includes this weekend. Chris, you're going to be part of this, too," Mom said, turning to Chris, who immediately wiped the smirk off his face and tried to look serious and mature.

"I will?" Chris' expression lit up, and Abi knew he was probably imagining the different ways he would torture her. *Of course, I just had to jinx it.*

"I wouldn't get too excited if I were you. This weekend I'm going to be at a seminar, and your father will be staying late at work. Since I know that if I leave Abi home alone, there is no way she will follow the rules I've set for her grounding—"

"Yes I would!" Abi interjected. "I'm a good kid!"

"Yeah, right!" Chris scoffed.

"—you're going to have to watch Abi."

"Gre—wait, wait a second. You mean I have to *babysit* her after school? For a whole week?" Chris groaned. "She's sixteen! She can take of herself! Besides, what about *my* plans?"

Abi laughed inwardly at his sudden willingness to defend her independence.

"I warned you not to get too excited," Mom said. "Besides, I think this will be some long overdue bonding time."

Chris glanced at his sister and frowned. Abi felt the same way. They got along well enough in spite of Chris's constant teasing, but "bonding time" was stretching their relationship.

"The way you children fight, you'd think you were enemies," Mrs. Candial continued. "You need to learn to get along, because family should be the strongest bond there is."

Abi sucked in her breath. An eerie foreboding came over her, as if the casually spoken words had actually been meant as a warning.

Well, then, that settles it. If that "strong bond" is tested, I'm doomed.

The Gate

"I have heard rumors of a man who has come into Meynch," a girl whispered to the group of women were clustered around her. They wore plain dresses, a mark of their lower status, and carried various sized containers as they all drew water from the well. "Are they true? Have you heard of this man, the Stranger?"

"The rumors are true," a stooped, gray-haired woman replied. "The man is certainly causing a stir. For one thing, Meynch has not had visitors since my parents were children and the ambassador from Maragor crossed the mountains to sign the peace treaty."

"That's not all that's strange about him," another woman interjected. "He's the man who walked right into Lara's house and demanded to spend the night there!" The dour-faced matron crossed her arms and scowled at the unfazed reactions she was receiving. "The audacity! An unmarried man spending the night with an unmarried woman, who has a young sister, no less! It's a violation of the law!"

The girls shrugged, not as scandalized as the matron obviously expected them to be. She huffed and, picking up her pitcher, she looked down her nose at them and stormed away.

"The lawmen are pretty upset about it too, I've heard." Another girl entered the conversation, and the women made room for her to draw water next to them. "Apparently he's been doing other things that are against the law too."

"Lara *did* say nothing happened between them. He just needed a place to stay the night, and all the inns were full. She said he asked several other people before he came to her, but they had all rejected him. And he's made it very clear that he's not the kind of man to take advantage of a girl."

"I don't believe it for a moment. If put into a situation with a willing woman, which I have no doubt there are plenty of, since he's charming but claims he's unavailable, every man becomes that kind of man, no matter how noble his intentions."

The others nodded, murmuring, "Sad, but true," as they filled their containers.

"Good morning, ladies," a pleasant voice said behind them, and they turned to see the subject of their discussion. "Could you please tell me the way to Kesan's house?"

"Go to the edge of town and keep walking until you see the house with the blue roof, and then take a left into the Area of the Merchants. Kesan's house is the first house on the right," the girl who had just insulted his morals replied.

The older women looked on, their eyes chilly with suspicion, but most of the younger girls studied him and found nothing to merit distrust. Though he was square-jawed and bright-eyed, he was not particularly handsome. He did not smile and try to charm them, or let his gaze flick over them and then dismiss them as insignificant like many other men did. His kind expression and honest air invited confidance and trust.

As he left, another girl came to them and saw him walk away. "He may be a criminal in the lawmen's eyes, but I've seen him and listened to him speak, and he doesn't seem that bad to me. Besides, he is the talk of the town! I would give anything for him to stay with me," she commented. The other girls quickly shushed their friend and walked away, giggling. The women just shook their heads, their disapproval clear.

"Abi? Abi, wake up!" Someone shook her shoulder.

"Huh? What?" Abi yawned and rubbed her eyes only to see Chris already dressed and wearing an annoying smirk. She closed her eyes again. "Go away," she said drowsily.

In response, Chris jerked off the covers.

Abi's eyes flew open at the loss of warmth, and she glared fiercely at her brother and then threw a quick look at the clock on her dresser. "It's only eight thirty… *and* it's a Saturday! As in, the weekend. As in, let me sleep in because there is no school!"

"Come on!" Chris opened Abi's closet and sifted through the outfits until he found a T-shirt and a pair of faded jeans, and he tossed them on her bed.

Abi threw her pillow at him. "Stop going through my closet!"

"Why? Do you have any pictures of boys in here?" Chris asked.

"No!" *As if there were any to put in there in the first place, which you know.*

"I thought so. Mom said I can't let you out of my sight, and I usually wake up about now, so you have to wake up, too."

"You're such a jerk! You have never woken up this early on a weekend in your entire life!" Abi moaned. "Why are you determined to torture me?" She pulled the blanket over her head in a vain attempt to pretend he didn't exist. *I am an only child. I am an only child,* she repeated to herself.

"Since when is waking up a little early torture?" When she did not respond, Chris sat on the bed and started bouncing, shaking the mattress violently.

"Ugh! You are so cruel!" Abi tried to kick him, but he held her feet together.

"All right! Fine, I'm getting up!" Abi sat up and swung her legs over the side of the bed. "Give me some privacy so I can get ready." Before he could get up, she pushed her brother until he fell off the bed, landing with a thump on his rear end. "That's for being such a jerk!"

He shrugged, unrepentant. "That's what I'm for." He stood up and dusted himself off. Abi immediately started pushing him toward her door. "Hurry up," was all he could add before Abi slammed the door in his face.

Ten minutes later, Abi threw open the door, letting it bang against the wall. Her eyes still sparked with irritation, though more subdued than earlier. "Now, since you woke me up, you have to think of something for us to do. And it better be something worth waking up this early for."

Chris raised an eyebrow. "Okay…so why don't we hang out in the backyard? You can bring a book to read, and I'll—"

"—stay with me. Remember, Mom said you have to keep an eye on me, and you can't do that if you're going to go hang out with your big, tough, jock guy friends oh-so-far away." Abi realized her chance for revenge and milked it for all it was worth.

"I wasn't going to go hang out with my friends!" Chris growled in a way that told Abi that he was going to do exactly that. "At least, not yet," he added under his breath.

"Payback is tough, isn't it?" And with that, Abi skipped back into her bedroom to get her book, then tossed a triumphant smile to her brother as she started toward the kitchen and opened the back door.

I honestly think the sole reason for little sisters is to bug the rest of us, Chris thought as he reluctantly followed Abi out into their backyard. *Yep, I'm pretty sure that's it. She's always doing weird stuff, like leave planet Earth in the middle of school, and everyone's like, "Oh, she's* your *sister?" And then they pity me or, worse, expect me to do the same things she does. Now she's in trouble and, as usual, guess whose social life also has to suffer for it?*

I guess it could be worse. She could be making me watch some corny chick flick with her. Chris shuddered at the thought. He looked up and saw how clear the sky was, and felt the cool breeze, and he added mentally, *And it is nice outside.*

He looked around their backyard. It was small but, as a result of their mother's knack for gardening, filled with all sorts of plant life. Two big oak trees stood guard on either side of the yard, and a small, stone-paved sidewalk carved a path between beautiful flowers and ferns. Birds perched in various trees, scattered across the yard, were singing, signalling the coming of the morning. Under a particularly large tree was a small porch swing that was old and worn, and its white paint was peeling. Abi moved toward it, but Chris hesitated for a moment. He sighed and stared longingly at his skateboard propped against the wall, but went to sit next to Abi.

They sat in silence for only a short while, but it seemed like an eternity to Chris. He occasionally peeked at Abi, but she was deeply absorbed in her book.

Chris breathed in deeply and slouched in the seat. He wished he had his iPod, but he had left it last weekend at his friend's house and never gotten it back. Bored, he tapped his fingers on the armrest of the porch swing.

The fresh, cool morning air was soothing, so much so that, against his will, Chris was starting to doze off, until he was interrupted by Abi's voice exclaiming, "Hey, Chris, I've never seen those stairs before."

Chris was about to ask, "What stairs?" when suddenly he noticed that a few yards away from the oak on the opposite side of the sidewalk, two trees seemed to form an arch over a staircase. He squinted, trying to look closer, and saw that it seemed to lead to raised ground, but it was too far away to tell.

What? Where did that come from? Am I going crazy? He blinked, rubbed his eyes, and looked again. *Nope. Still there. How in the world did a random staircase appear in our backyard overnight? There's no way it could have been there yesterday. I think I would have noticed if it were.*

Maybe I never really woke up this morning. Maybe this is all a dream.

Chris gripped the side of the porch swing, and a splinter jabbed into his palm. "Oww!" *So, this is* not *a dream.* He glanced over at his sister. She obviously had seen it, too, which meant he was not hallucinating.

Why don't you go explore? A voice inside him prodded.

Why would I do that? I don't know what's up there. It could be dangerous. I should just stay here and blow it off, tell Abi it's no big deal.

But this might be your only chance to actually do *something instead of sitting around, being bored out of your mind. Honestly, you're overthinking this. Just go. What's the worst that can happen? You find out nothing's up there, you can come right back down and pretend like it never happened.*

You know what? Chris thought. *Why not?*

"I've never seen it before, either," he said aloud. "Why don't we explore what's up there?" For a moment, Chris was surprised at the fact that he had actually said it; then he gathered up his courage and repeated, "Come on, let's go look around."

"Why?" was Abi's annoyingly logical question.

"Well…" He gauged her emotions from her face. She seemed to be geniunely curious, but the problem with his sister was that she was much more cautious than he was, and there was no way she was going to go if he said his motivation was just boredom and a voice in his head. In fact, she'd probably call him nuts. "Well…does there have to be a *why*? I mean, can't we just go for the fun of it? If there's nothing up there, we can always come right back down."

Abi glanced at him, then at the stairs with a strange expression on her face, then looked back down at her book. "Nah. I want to finish my book first. Maybe later."

Chris felt oddly disappointed, and yet he somehow knew that if he went, she would come, too. So he made a quick decision. "See you up there!" And with that, Chris sprinted to the trees, ducked under the low-hanging branches, and ran up the steps out of sight.

"Hey, Abi, come up he—!"

Abi's head jerked up as his words abruptly were cut off. "What?" she yelled and then listened for a response.

Nothing.

"Chris, come on. Stop joking around and get down here."

Still nothing.

"Chris?" Her voice was higher pitched now, frantic. Abi put down her book, her worry increasing. Without even thinking, her gut told her something had happened to Chris. Even though he was sometimes a jerk, he would have come out by now, yelling, "Gotcha!" if this was a prank. He wouldn't drag it out this long. He wouldn't worry her like this on purpose.

But she really didn't want to go up the stairs after him. Yes, she had pointed them out to Chris, but she had not expected him to do anything about it. For all she knew, her parents had asked someone to put them in their backyard while they were at school.

Then why haven't I seen them before?

There's no other logical explanation. It's not as if stairs can appear out of thin air…right? That would be like something out of Harry Potter. *And that stuff isn't real, is it?*

But what if he's in trouble? Or hurt? As annoying as he is, he's still my brother! I can't leave him up there with who knows what just because I'm afraid of some stupid stairs!

As if it was a sign, a ray of sunlight appeared suddenly and shone directly on the staircase that loomed in front of her. Looking around, she saw her dad's flashlight on the ground by her brother's skateboard and picked it up. If she was going to enter a shadowy, creepy-looking staircase, she might as well have a flashlight.

She directed the beam of her flashlight to the top of the staircase. All she could see were more stairs, for the dark shade of large oak trees blocked the rest from her view. Walking around the staircase, she realized with a start that the stairs were hovering in midair. There was nothing beneath them—no support if she fell through.

I can do this. I can walk up those stairs. By myself. Without knowing what, or who, is up there. Abi's breathing quickened, and she felt like her heart was about to pound out of her chest. *Okay, so maybe I can't do this. But Chris is up there. I can't just leave him there!*

Abi swallowed hard. *Chris, I'm so going to kill you if this is your idea of a joke.*

Abi held the flashlight in front of her like a weapon then slowly ascended the mysterious staircase. At about every other step, she turned her head to look at the ground, longing to go back and forget this ever happened. Or at least wake up and find this was all a strange dream. But she kept walking.

Almost moments later, she reached solid ground. *Wait a second. The stairs were huge! How did I get to the top so fast?* She looked around.

She stood on a small plateau that was dotted with clumps of grass but was mostly sandy and barren. Most importantly, there was no sign of Chris.

And then she saw it. It was an large, ordinary-looking wooden gate on the other end of the flat terrain. It was opened a little already, which meant…

"Chris went through the gate!"

Wait a minute. Calm down. It's a gate. It probably leads to the other side, Abi reasoned to herself. But she could plainly see the gate was at the very edge of the plateau, and that if it led to the other side, Chris would have just fallen off the staircase, and she would have seen him on the ground below.

She put her flashlight on the ground and walked over to the gate, looking through the crack. Blazing white light shone through the gap. She stared at the gate. *What is going on?* Abi thought. An unnatural silence filled the air around her as if the world around her was holding its breath.

"Go in," a still, small voice whispered in Abi's ear, quiet and solemn and firm. "Go in."

What am I waiting for? I need to find my brother. What would I say to Mom if I left him wherever he is? I can see the conversation now.

"Where's Chris?"

"Oh, sorry, Mom, but Chris went up some weird stairs that appeared out of nowhere, disappeared through this gate that took him who-knows-where, and may or may not be dead right now. But I was too scared to check it out, so I waited five hours until you got back to find him. Hey, when's dinner?" Yeah, that *would go over well. Grounding would seem like child's play compared to what she would to do me.*

I guess it wouldn't hurt to at least look. Right?

Abi slowly opened the door and stepped into the light.

Meynch

When Abi opened her eyes, she was greeted with the sight of huge, snow-capped mountains towering over her.

She blinked in shock, her head jerked, and she instinctively stepped back. She steadied herself quickly before she lost her balance and looked down. At the base of the mountain lay a picturesque town that was surrounded by trees. Looking closely, Abi could even see a castle at the top of the mountain. She took another step forward and fell head over heels down the grassy slope she had been standing on. She curled up into a ball as she rolled, trying to protect her face, until she bumped into a rock and abruptly came to a stop.

"Ow!" Abi stood up and brushed herself off, gingerly touching several bruises on her arms and back. "I'm sure not in my backyard anymore." Realization dawned on her, and she turned to look behind her. She gasped.

The gate was gone!

"Abi! I was wondering when you would get here."

Abi whirled around to see Chris sitting on a boulder nearby, his eyes dancing as he watched her expression change. She stormed over to him, and he could almost see the smoke coming out of her ears.

"Chris, this better not be some sort of prank. Because I promise, if I wasn't so afraid of what Mom would do to me if I didn't bring you home fully intact..."

She left the sentence hanging, the threat in her voice clear. "You're a jerk of the first order, for putting me through that. We need to go home. Now. Where did the gate go?"

"What do you mean, where did the…" Chris stared at the hill that Abi had fallen down. There was no sign of a gate; in fact, the hill looked completely barren.

"You really don't know where the gate went?" Abi was starting to panic, and as her alarm increased, so did her anger. "Chris, if this is a prank, I am going to hurt you so badly!" She paused at Chris' smirk. "Well, I'll at least get Mom on your case so fast your head will spin!"

"Abi, let's be honest here. You couldn't hurt a fly. And I'm flattered that you think I could snap my fingers and make the gate disappear, just like that. But really? You know me better than that. I'm an ordinary, Adonis-looking, buff male specimen with no magical abilities whatsoever except for my smile."

Abi snorted, then frowned. "Then why do you look so happy?" she asked irritably.

He grinned. "You have to admit, this is much better than sitting around and doing nothing at home."

"Oh, yeah, *now* we're sitting around and doing nothing *and* we have no idea where we are!" Abi clenched her fists, getting ready to tear into her brother. "You are such a idiot! How could you just ignore every single safety lesson you've ever learned? Now who knows where we are, or what kind of danger you've gotten us into—"

A voice interrupted her tirade. "There's no need to work yourself up. Meynch is a harmless little town."

"Who said that?" Chris asked, unconsciously putting his arm around Abi in a protective gesture. Abi hit his arm away, still furious with him, and looked for the source of the voice.

"I did. Turn around."

Abi and Chris turned around to see a handsome face peek out from behind another rock. Then a young man walked out from behind it and into view. He looked about Chris's age, with curly dark hair and bluish-gray eyes. He had on a robe tied around his trim waist and pants underneath.

Chris wasn't sure if they were in some alien world, but this guy didn't look much like aliens he had seen in comic books and movies. *He looks normal enough, but his clothes are definitely out of date. They look like something from medieval times,* Chris thought.

"What is this 'medieval?' Shall I take that as a compliment?" the young man asked. His voice was cheerful, and his eyes were mischievous.

"What?" Chris said, startled. "I didn't say anything." One look at Abi's laughing eyes, though, told him he spoke his thoughts out loud.

The boy grinned at Chris's embarrassment and turned to Abi. "So is *medieval* a compliment or an insult? And is your boyfriend always this transparent?"

"Well, medieval is a little bit of both. And unfortunately, he's my brother. If he was my boyfriend, I could get rid of him," Abi joked, but seeing Chris's scowl, put up her hands in mock surrender and asked the boy, "Can I ask you a couple questions?"

"Ask away."

"Who are you, where are we, and how did we get here?"

The guy looked at Abi curiously, studying her as he formed his reply. "I really wish I could help you, but I can only answer some of your questions. My name is Nathan, and you are on the outskirts of the town of Meynch. How you got here, I cannot say, for you seemed to appear out of the air." He grinned, and Abi decided he was cute, especially with those dimples.

Don't get too excited, Abi warned herself. *For one, for all we know, we've been transported to Mars or something, and this Nathan guy is an alien. And besides, the really cute guys are always taken. That's a universal rule;...even if we are on another planet.*

"Nathan! Boy, where are you?" a loud voice called from the valley.

Nathan took Abi's hand and touched his lips to her knuckles. She blushed. "Excuse me, I must go, for that is my master," Nathan said quickly. "May the Shepherd King grant me the pleasure of seeing you again!"

Then he hurried off without a look back.

Abi and Chris sat in silence for a while, and then Abi got up and started walking toward the valley.

"Hey, Abi, wait up!" Chris said, hurrying to catch up with her. "Where are you going?"

"Since you dragged me out here, and we can't get back because the gate is gone, I might as well make the best of it." Her dreamy expression, though, belied her words.

"Oh yeah, like that's your only reason."

Abi whirled around to face him. "What are you suggesting?"

Chris mimicked Nathan's deep, courteous tone. "May the Shepherd grant me the *pleasure* of seeing you again!" He switched to his normal tone and rolled his eyes. "He was so obviously flirting with you. I was about to gag all over him when he kissed your hand. I mean, we're definitely in some sort of medieval world, and in his mind, you're his 'fair lady,'" he said mockingly.

Abi blushed, but tried to keep her voice even and indifferent. "Shut up. Mind your own business."

"Fine, but I wonder what Dad will say about some alien guy flirting with his daughter, especially since he already has a problem when regular guys flirt with you."

"You wouldn't tell. Besides, we don't even know if…"

"…we can even *get* back home." Chris sobered faster than she had ever seen him before. "You're right." He looked at her, noticing the darkening spots on her bare arms for the first time. "What happened to your arms?"

Abi glanced at her arms. "Oh, I fell when I came out of the gate and rolled for a bit. Good thing I did gymnastics last summer, right? At least I'm not totally out of shape."

Chris shook his head. "Geez, Abi, I'm sorry. I should have waited for you before going through the gate."

Oh my gosh, he admitted I was right about something and *apologized! This is a day for the records!* Abi bit her tongue to keep from speaking her thoughts.

"We have no idea where we are, and Mom and Dad will probably be worried sick," Chris continued. "We're definitely not in Kansas anymore, Toto." He cracked a small smile, but it quickly disappeared.

He firmed his jaw, and Abi saw the beginnings of something she had never seen in her brother before: focused determination. "If going to this Meynch place means we can find a way to go back, you're right. We need to go. Now."

What Not to Wear in Meynch

As Abi and Chris approached the valley, Abi's mind drifted…

The women she had seen before were gathered again at the well. This time, they didn't even have water pitchers with them, making it clear that their sole purpose was to gossip.

"Can you believe the Stranger's boldness? He has admitted, in public to basically the whole town, that he believes he is the son of the Shepherd!"

"That's blasphemy! The law says a man must have proof of such an absurd claim!"

"Well, he has none but his word, and *still* people believe him."

"Just goes to show how gullible people are. No one's heard from the Shepherd King in years! There are rumors that he died long ago, or that he didn't even exist in the first place."

"I've heard the rumors too. They're nothing new. For all the people that believe in this Stranger, there are just as many waiting for an opprotunity to seize power, now that it's clear the King is not going to act directly."

"Shh! Look, here comes the Stranger now!"

The ladies smiled sweetly as the man walked by, hardly seeing them. His expression was angry and frustrated and sad all at the same time.

"I wonder what his problem is. He came from the direction of the courthouse. I've heard he's made a lot of enemies there."

"If the lawmen simply disliked him before, they definitely hate him with a passion now. But everyone else loves him. He gives them hope."

"That's worse for him. The lawmen are getting insanely jealous. He'll need all his wits about him if he's going to keep from getting arrested now. They'll do whatever they think is necessary to trip him up. They'll bribe every person in the whole town of Meynch if they have to."

"Abi? Abi, snap out of it!"

"Huh? What?" Abi said dazedly.

"You were walking, and then all of a sudden you stopped and sat down and stared at the valley," Chris said, looking concerned.

Abi reached out and gripped Chris's arm tightly. "Chris, listen. Ever since yesterday, this sort of thing has been happening to me. I've been seeing people I don't even know in these weird daydreams that I thought I was making up, but I'm starting to think that they're real."

"Abi, be serious. I mean, I know you live in la-la land but this is a bit much. You know your daydreams aren't real."

Abi felt a pang of hurt that he had just basically echoed the mocking taunts she had heard constantly at school, but pushed it aside. "Yes, obviously most of my daydreams aren't real, but in what I just saw a moment ago, the people were talking about the town of Meynch. And isn't that where Nathan said we needed to go?" She looked up at Chris from her position on the grass.

Chris looked down at her doubtfully. Abi's heart sank. "You don't believe me," she said quietly.

Chris raised an eyebrow. "You might have been subconsciously putting what Nathan told you in your daydream. Besides them talking about Meynch, what makes this daydream any different from the other ones you always have?"

"I just…have a feeling. I can't explain it. But honestly, I am really convinced that whatever I'm seeing really happened, and it has to do with this place, Meynch." She paused and searched her brother's gaze. "I don't blame you for not believing me. I'm not sure *I* even believe me. This whole situation is so insane!"

Abi saw the exact moment Chris shifted from outright disbelief to shaky acceptance. Reaching out his hand, Chris lifted Abi to her feet. "I believe you. Sort of. I had the same sort of gut feeling that told me to climb the stairs, so I see where you're coming from. It's more than a little crazy, but so is being magically transported to another world or dimension or wherever the heck we are. Crazy seems to be becoming more and more normal here."

Abi sighed and shrugged. "I guess some belief is enough, for now. At least until we get some answers."

It felt like Abi and Chris had walked several miles when they finally entered the town of Meynch, stepping through a large arch that was covered with vines.

Chris looked around curiously. Everything looked so…old-fashioned. There was one wide dirt road that branched off at seemingly random places. He could see no modern-looking buildings, not even a suburban townhouse. Instead, the houses around him were large and appeared to have at least two floors and an open roof. Trees and flowers surrounded the entrance to each home. The effect was pretty but unusual.

Abi noticed a cute, blond-haired boy who held his mother's hand as they walked down the road, and when she made eye contact with him, she smiled kindly.

The boy whispered loudly, "Mommy, why are they dressed funny?"

Abi blushed and looked away, avoiding the curious gaze of both mother and child. "Chris, maybe we should try to blend in a little more," Abi whispered to her brother as they walked. "We stick out like sore thumbs. Everyone's dressed differently than us. If people as weirdly dressed as they apparently think we are came up to me and asked me questions like 'Where am I?' and 'What am I doing here?,' I would be too busy calling 911 and backing away to help them." She looked down at her jeans and T-shirt and then at the old-fashioned dresses and tunics.

"You're right. All we're here to do is find out why we're here and how we can go home. It's probably not a good idea to draw attention to ourselves." Chris looked around. He spotted a small building that looked just like all the other homes except for the sign in its window. "There's some sort of store. 'Kesan's Garments.'" He turned to Abi. "Why don't we go inside and see if we can get some new clothes? Maybe that will help make us more inconspicuous."

"Okay, that sounds like a good idea."

Chris grinned. "Yeah, I have those a lot."

Abi tapped her finger against her chin and looked at him askance. "Let's see…whose crazy idea was it to climb the stairs and go through the gate?"

"Uhhh…"

She smirked. "I thought so."

The merry tinkle of the bell hanging over the door signaled their arrival as Abi and Chris entered the shop. As they viewed the interior, they stood in the doorway, shocked at the sight that greeted them.

One side of the shop was filled with khaki-looking pants and normal T-shirts, but it was labeled *Undergarments*. The other side was filled with solid-colored robes and tunics that looked like they came straight out of a medieval peasant village and was labeled *Outer garments*.

"Umm…I think the reason we got weird looks is because they think we're walking around in our underwear," Abi mumbled.

As they stood there, a burly man with curly, sandy blond hair came up to them. "Hello, lad!" he said loudly, slapping Chris on the back. "How can I help you? Wait, don't answer that," he said quickly, looking him over, "for I can see plainly what you need. You've been walking around in your underclothes!"

Then Kesan noticed Abi. "Lass, why, you are in your under clothes, too!" His amusement disappeared as he studied them, and his face became disapproving. "You both are much too young to be in such an relationship."

Blushing furiously once she realized what he thought, Abi immediately spoke up. "No, I can explain. This isn't how it looks." *Oh wow, if I wasn't so confused, I would be creeped out that this guy thinks I'm with Chris. Eew.* "This is my brother and we are from…out of town. Where we come from, what we are wearing is appropriate clothing. We didn't know that it was different here."

Kesan looked skeptical but apparently decided to accept her explanation. "Well, let me get your measurements, and I'll find you some new attire," he said as he got out a rolled up piece of cloth. When he unrolled it, she saw that it had lines and numbers for measurement, like a tape measure.

All of a sudden, Abi remembered something. *In the dream I had the other day, Kesan was the name of the man who that Stranger guy wanted to find!*

So I was *dreaming about Meynch! It* is *real! It was some sort of…foresight, or vision. That's it, I'm having visions!* She took a second look at the shopkeeper, and her mind spun with possible theories. *Is it coincidence that Kesan is the first person we met in Meynch? Does the reason we were brought here have something to do with him, or the Stranger?*

But her thoughts were interrupted when Kesan held up a strapless, knee-length turquoise dress. It was definitely a far cry from the plain dresses of the women she had seen at the well in her vision. "Lass, you are in luck. Your measurements are the same as another wealthy young lady who came in yesterday. And I have a dress that she didn't like that may fit you. Look, it's even the exact same shade as your beautiful eyes!"

Abi practically salivated at the sight of the beautiful dress. *Oooh, that dress is absolutely stunning! But I have so many questions that I should be asking… Well, they can wait until I try on the dress, right? After all, we do need to be inconspicuous if we're going to blend in and try to find a way home.*

After a moment's hesitation, Abi took it from Kesan's hands, and her trepidation was put aside as she inspected the dress. *Really, can anyone blame me? I* am *a girl, first and foremost, and, as a girl, I am naturally drawn to cute guys and cute outfits. And this outfit is gor-geous! I'll just try it on really quickly.*

"And for the young man…" Kesan sifted through a sack of robes on the shelf and finally chose a short-sleeved, chocolate-brown robe. "Here, take this." He gave the robe to Chris, as well as a white undershirt and khaki pants. "The dressing room is in the back of the shop. Try them on, and if they don't fit, I can adjust them as needed."

"But we can't pay you," Chris protested. "We don't have any money."

"We'll discuss your payment later." Kes smiled, but his gaze was narrow and intent as he watched them walk away.

KESAN'S ADVICE

Abi twirled in front of the full-length mirror on the wall. The ruffled hem of the robe, embroidered with tiny flowers, flared around her hips. "This dress is gorgeous!"

Chris grinned. "Nathan won't be able to take his eyes off of you. My little sister is dressed to impress."

Abi blushed and immediately retorted, "Shut up! Stop trying to embarrass me. We probably won't even see him again."

When they returned to the front of the store, Kesan scrutinized their outfits carefully. "Yes, they fit well. I have a good eye for clothes, no? But I did not make them. My wife is an excellent seamstress. She is one of the best in town." He smiled.

Wait a second…his smile looks familiar. Abi frowned.

"Is something wrong?" Chris asked.

Abi opened her mouth and then glanced at Kesan. She couldn't say anything with him there. Besides, it was just a hunch. She needed proof. "Uh, no. Just trying to figure out how we can pay you back for the clothes."

The shopkeeper's eyes narrowed, though he still had the smile on his face. "Yes…payment. Come with me to the back room, and we will discuss an arrangement."

Now Abi was becoming wary. "Be careful," she whispered to Chris. "It's not exactly safe to walk into a secluded room with a complete stranger."

"So far he seems to mean us no harm," Chris replied. "But you're right. I doubt everyone here is trustworthy. At the first sign of trouble, we leave."

Kesan led them into a small room, with Abi and Chris looking around cautiously. "Sit down," he said, motioning to a modest table and chairs.

Once they sat down, Kesan sat down beside them. "Lass, you were right to be suspicious, although I assure you I intend you no harm. You are strangers in Meynch, and because of that, you already have enemies, whether you know it or not. You also are young and do not know the way of things here, and far worse people than I will seek to take advantage of you." He saw their puzzled expressions and tried to explain further. "I'm going too fast, aren't I? Let me start from the beginning. Meynch is made up of four groups of people."

"You mean like upper class, middle class, lower class sort of thing?" Chris asked.

"It's not as simple as that, although there are definitely many similarities, or at least there were. Those with the highest authority are the lawmen. They consider themselves to be above the rest of the people. They're always at the courthouse, and they live, breathe, and eat the laws that were given to us by the Shepherd King. Some of them are honest in their attempts to enforce justice, but sadly many of them have become experienced in twisting the law for their own gain."

The Shepherd King... That's the guy Nathan mentioned! "Who's the Shepherd King?" Abi asked curiously.

Kesan rubbed his chin. "Actually, I can't tell you much about him. All I know is that he lives in the castle above the mountains of Troche. He hasn't come down in a very long time, although…" He paused. "But that's a story for another time. I am a merchant. We, that is, the merchants and shopkeepers, are wealthy, but in general, our reputation as dishonest precedes us. Few are trustworthy, and vendors in general are always viewed with suspicion by, well, pretty much everyone. Though I and a few others try to maintain our honor in our dealings, most of my rank are always looking to turn a profit and are willing to do just about anything to get rich. Many aid the lawmen by selling any knowledge they have. Some even go so low as to trade with Maragor, the barbaric town beyond the mountains of Troche." He paused, checking if Abi and Chris were keeping up.

Abi and Chris nodded to show they were still listening. However, it was not lost on them that Kesan had effectively dodged the topic of the Shepherd King.

"The lawmen and the merchants are a minority in Meynch. The majority of Meynch are just average, hard-working people trying to make a living for themselves and their families as blacksmiths, farmers, stable owners, and the like. But make sure to watch out for a lady named Pilandra. She can spread gossip faster than a wildfire spreads on dry ground, and she works closely with the lawmen. The merest hint of anything unusual or radical going on, and you can be sure she will tell them.

"And last but not least, the strangers. Before the Stranger came five years ago, there were only three groups of people, much like your idea of upper, middle, and lower classes. But the Stranger didn't fit into any of those groups. Since his impact on our town was irreversible and undeniable, the lawmen had to make a category for him, so now whoever passes through town is a stranger. And since the lawmen hated the Stranger more than anything, they now hate all strangers. Any questions?"

"Mr. Kesan, sir…" Abi spoke up.

"Just Kes, please."

"Okay. Kes, who is the Stranger? What did he do to get the lawmen to hate all strangers? And why is He *the* Stranger? Why is He just not *a* stranger?"

Kes smiled. "You are very perceptive. To answer your many questions, I would have to tell you a story that has so many different layers that it would take days to tell it completely. Even then, it probably wouldn't be enough. But what I can tell, I will, if you do me a little favor."

Chris's eyes narrowed. "Like what?"

Kes leaned forward. "Tell me the truth. Where are you from? Where are your parents? I know that there is much to your story that you don't want to tell, and I don't blame you for being hesitant. But I have, I hope, proven that I can be trusted."

Abi bit her lip. "Yes, you have…but I don't think you'll believe us if we told you."

Kes propped his chin in his hand. "Try me."

After thirty minutes of Abi trying to explain her life to Kes and Chris's constant interruptions, Kes raised his eyebrows in disbelief.

"You expect me to believe that you came from *another world*?"

"Believe what you want," Chris said, standing up. "But if you don't even know what Earth is, I'd say we are from different dimensions at the very least."

Kes sighed. "All right, all right. I see no reason for you to lie. It's certainly not in your best interests for me to think you're crazy. But you are going to have to give me some time to absorb this."

"Trust me," Chris said, "we know how you feel. You think this is easy for us to take in? I'm still hoping that, any moment now, my alarm's going to go off and wake me up. But if this is real, that means that we just walked into another dimension completely by accident. And since it's not like we stroll into other dimensions every day, this is more than a little freaky to us."

The shopkeeper flashed a tentative smile and changed the subject. "I suppose you don't have a place to stay?"

Abi and Chris shook their heads.

"I thought so. You probably didn't call ahead and make reservations at the inn." He laughed at his own joke. "You can stay with me and my family for now. Let me introduce you to my family. Marla, Nathan, Weana, come here, please!" Kes called.

Chris nudged Abi. "Nathan?" he whispered, a small smile tugging at the corners of his mouth.

"There are lots of Nathans in the world," Abi said, her cheeks reddening.

"You mean *our* world. But I highly doubt there are that many here," Chris said in a sing-song voice, his smile now a full-blown grin.

A lady came, holding a small child. Nathan followed behind them, and when he saw Abi, he grinned slyly.

Kes started introducing them. "Marla, Nathan, Weana, this is Abi and Chris. Children, this is my wife, Marla, and my daughter, Weana, and this is Nathan—"

Nathan interrupted and bowed. "It's all right. I believe we've already met."

No one noticed Abi's pink cheeks, which got even redder when he raised his head and winked at her.

The Information Center

Chris shook hands with Nathan, giving him the macho older brother look. Instead of reacting or having some sort of male dominance routine, Nathan simply met Chris's gaze evenly.

Abi groaned mentally. *Thank God for that. At least someone here has patience, because I'm about to lose mine. Chris only decides to be the protective older brother when it suits him, and when is that? When he knows that it will annoy me the most. Like scaring away one of the few guys that has even shown some sign of interest in me. Even if he's an alien.*

Kes motioned for everyone to sit down at the table.

"We kept our part of the bargain, now you keep yours," Chris said quietly to Kesan. "You promised you would tell us about the Stranger."

"You what!" Marla exclaimed, anger instantly turning her face a bright cherry red. "You know what the lawmen would do to us if we even talk about the Stranger with each other, let alone with other strangers! We'll be arrested and executed!"

"Honey—" Kes started, trying to console her.

"Don't 'honey' me! I'm not putting the lives of our family in danger for *strangers*!"

"Now that's enough, woman!" Kes thundered. "They have just as much right to the truth as we do!"

Nathan and Weana were stunned. They had never seen Kes yell at his wife.

"They're *strangers*," Marla retorted. "Why should we care what they do?"

"But they're just children!"

"Yes, they're children. Naïve, young *strangers* who don't know how the lawmen can make their lives miserable!"

As their argument went on, Chris tapped Abi on the shoulder. "We've already worn out our welcome here," he whispered to her. "It's time to go."

Abi and Chris tiptoed outside, closing the door gently behind them.

Nathan watched them go, a strange gleam in his eye.

"I guess we'll never know about the Stranger." Abi sighed sadly as she walked alongside Chris. "But it's so weird what Marla said about those lawmen people making our lives miserable. I mean, we're strangers, right? They can't do anything to us because we're not under their laws."

Chris shrugged and looked at the ground. "I guess. I don't get it, though. This whole place doesn't seem like anything from a sci-fi movie where they've been 'transported to another dimension.' They don't speak another language, and besides the different clothes, they seem like people we would meet on Earth." Chris lifted his head and stared at the sky. "What kind of crazy world are we in?" he thought aloud.

Abi could not answer him, so they walked in silence for a while. "So how do we find out who the Stranger is and what he has to do with us being able to go home?" Abi asked.

"I don't know. Wait!" Chris exclaimed. "Do you see that house over there?" He pointed to a small cottage on the other side of the road. It was the very picture of a haunted house; the paint on the door and shutters was peeling, and the wood appeared rustic and old. But the sign beside it said, "Information Center" in bold, black letters, and there was a faint silhouette in the window. "I bet the guy in there knows."

"Wait a second…an information center? Don't they only have those in malls, for customer service and stuff? That seems a little weird to have in the middle of a town."

"Yeah, it's a little strange, but this whole place is strange. Do you have a better idea?" When Abi didn't answer, Chris nodded, satisfied. "Let's just check it out."

They walked quickly toward the cottage and rang the doorbell.

"Come in," a quiet voice said.

They opened the door and walked inside. The house's appearance was deceiving, or so it seemed. Inside, it was elaborately decorated with fine Persian rugs, amber curtains with intricate designs, and furniture of beautiful cherry-colored wood.

"Hello?" Chris called. When he heard no reply, he again shouted, "Hello? Is anyone here?" But there was still no answer.

Abi was staring straight ahead at the room in front of them. "Chris…"

He turned to look at his sister in puzzlement. "I wonder whose voice we heard."

"Chris, look in front—"

"And who was the guy we saw through the window?"

"*Chris!*"

He frowned at her. "What? What's wrong?"

"Look in front of you!"

Chris looked straight into the eyes of a phantom.

"Ahh!" Chris screamed and started running toward the door. After a while, he noticed he hadn't moved, that he was staring at the wall, and that Abi held the back of his robe as a grin spread across her face. She started laughing, and he realized she was laughing at *him*.

"Let go of me! Come on, we've got to get out of here! I saw a ghost!"

"Really, Chris? Are you serious? That's your shadow on the wall," Abi said when her laughter died down.

Chris looked at the wall and, sure enough, there was his shadow, enlarged and misshapen because of how the light from the window reflected off him.

"Oh." Embarrassed, Chris stepped away from Abi. "I knew that."

"Ri-ight." Abi's eyes danced with laughter. "You're such an idiot. That's who I was trying to show you," she said, pointing to a man sitting on a couch. His head was bent over a book, and he was reading it intently, apparently unaware of his visitors' presence.

Well, on the bright side, at least it doesn't look like he saw or heard that *embarrassing little episode,* Chris thought.

"Uh, excuse me, sir," Abi said hesitantly.

The bent head snapped up and looked at them. "How may I help you?"

The man was well-built and muscular, with a smiling face and shoulder-length black hair. Chris could tell, even though he was sitting, that he was very tall. His smooth hands told of an easy life, his pale skin of not much exposure to sun, and his ice-blue eyes sent shivers up and down Chris's spine. But to Abi, something in them looked strangely familiar.

"Do you know where to find the Stranger?" Abi asked.

The man studied them carefully, looking them up and down as if analyzing whether they were worth his time. Then he blinked as her question sunk in, his expression one of sheer horror before he quickly assumed a pleasant façade. Abi was not fooled.

He placed the book on the table in front of him and patted the seat beside him. "Sit down, sit down. You must be starving! Here, let me get you some food." And he disappeared into the hallway.

"He's hiding something," Abi said, keeping her voice soft just in case the man could overhear. "Even if he answers us, he's not going to tell us everything he knows."

"I agree," Chris replied. "At this point, I'll take some information over nothing. But we need to be on our guard."

Just then, the man walked in and gently placed two bowls of hot chicken soup in front of them.

"I'm afraid we haven't been introduced properly. What are your names?" the man said as he ate his soup.

"My name's…"

"Anna." Chris interrupted. "Her name's Anna. My name is…" Chris rolled his eyes upward and said, "David. My name is David."

The man looked at them so intently that Abi was afraid he could see through her brother's lie. "My name's Micah." He paused to slurp the remains of his soup. "Glad to have you join me. Now, about your question. Is there any particular reason for it?"

Chris was not about to tell him the truth. His eyes were too untrustworthy for Chris's liking, and Abi's warning was fresh in his mind. So instead he just shook his head. "No, not really. We're just curious," he lied.

"Hmm…" Micah murmured. "There's a saying, 'Curiosity killed the cats…or in this case, the kittens.'" He paused, letting them wonder whether that was a threat or a warning.

"We've heard that before," Abi said quietly. "Your point would be?"

"Oh, no point at all, simply an observation. But anyway, I think I have a book on the history of the last fifty years. Wait here," and he disappeared again.

"Chris!" Abi stood up, hands on her hips, once Micah had left.

"What?" Chris said innocently.

Abi rolled her eyes. "Don't try to weasel out of this one. Since when was my name Anna and your name David?"

Chris lowered his voice to a whisper. "Names mean identification. We didn't tell Kes our names, which means that if we just blend in as much as possible, we should be safe. The lawmen seem to be able to really make trouble for strangers. Micah just blatantly threatened us. We shouldn't draw attention to ourselves, and we shouldn't give anyone a way to identify and find us."

Before Abi could reply, Micah walked back in the room, carrying a huge book. "*The Chronicles of Meynch: Its Laws and History.*" He sat down and opened. "Here is written the story of the Stranger…"

The Stranger

"Not very long ago, a young man appeared in our small town. He claimed he had traveled the long and arduous road from the mountains to the town of Meynch to tell everyone that he was the King's son come to free them from the supposed burden of oppression the lawmen had upheld. For sixteen years he remained in Meynch. As the town became accustomed to the stranger in their midst, everyone formed their own opinions. The peasants loved him because he pretended to care about them and called them special. He even said he had the supposed power to heal people's sicknesses, and soon they began to bring their children to him in mobs that followed him everywhere. Others, like the merchants, simply tolerated him, because what he taught made the peasants more honest in their business dealings, and their trades thrived. The lawmen hated him because…" Micah smiled strangely. "Can you guess?"

"He changed their whole way of life, and since they were tyrants, they could not stop him because they knew he told the truth?" Abi offered.

"Uhh…yes. Of course." Micah nodded, but Chris saw him wince at the word *tyrants* before the older man concealed his expression. "So they eventually decided to lynch him. But unfortunately, he died of a heart attack before they could."

"But if he's dead, how can we go to him?" Chris asked.

"Nine days after he died, the lawmen came to check that the body was still in the coffin because they had heard rumors about the friends of the Stranger coming to honor the body. They found an empty grave.

"They assumed the friends took it. But the friends of the Stranger were asked if they knew where the body was, and they said they did not. And there were rumors of various eyewitnesses who saw the body *supposedly* alive."

Micah looked both of them in the eye. "To this day, no one knows what happened to his body. But his friends still spread the…" Micah seemed to restrain himself from saying something, "…message that the Stranger told them."

"So basically you're telling us that no one knows if the Stranger is still alive?" Chris's skepticism was clear.

"No, he's dead, all right. It's where the body is that no one knows," Micah retorted.

"Wow. Thanks for helping us. I mean, you were so clear in your explanation, an open book really. But this is a lot to take in. Can you please excuse us for a moment?" Chris asked.

"Certainly." Apparently missing the sarcasm in Chris' voice, Micah stood up and left the room.

Chris turned to his sister and shrugged. "Wow, that guy has issues! He's got the closed-off, creepily mysterious thing down pat. Anyway, that officially ends our search. The Stranger is dead. Time for a Plan B."

"Chris, I don't believe him. Something tells me we should keep looking. Obviously this Stranger guy had power, if he could heal people and stuff, whether Micah was willing to admit it or not."

"You mean like the magic from *Harry Potter* with the wands and the cloaks and flying broomsticks? Are you serious? Abi, you know magic isn't real. We're not going to find a horcrux in a chamber of secrets."

"Okay, first, Harry Potter didn't find the horcruxes in the chamber of secrets. Duh. And second, I think you're wrong. In our world, magic's not real. But maybe here, it is. The only person that can get us back home is someone who has enough power. And this Stranger seems to be our only option."

"Abi, if he died, he's dead."

"Obviously. But we can't get out of Meynch until the gate decides to reappear, or until we find someone who can make the gate reappear."

Chris studied Abi carefully, then sighed. "All right, but if we find out he's dead, we'll stop looking and wait for the gate to come back."

"Come on, this guy has power. He probably faked his own death or something, I don't know. But Chris, we were sent here for a purpose. I mean, you don't find a gate to another world every day. I don't know what that purpose is yet, but I do know, as of now, the only way to get home is to find the Stranger."

Abi and Chris got up and made as if to leave, but Micah came back and said, “Leaving so soon?”

“Yes,” Chris said, “our parents will be expecting us. But thank you, sir, for all your help.”

“Yes,” Abi agreed, “you’ve aided us very much. But we really must be going.” They walked toward the door.

“Wait!” Micah said. “Something tells me you’ll need this.” He handed them a scroll. “Do not open it until you find what you are looking for.”

Abi nodded and walked outside. Chris, on the other hand, held the scroll in his hand, looking suspiciously at it, then at Micah. *There’s no way I’m waiting that long to see what’s inside this thing*, Chris thought. *This guy isn’t telling us everything he knows, so why should we trust him?*

“Good-bye, Anna and David!” Micah called as they walked away.

When they were out of sight, Micah went back into his cottage and looked at the veiled window. “Rogan, you may come out now.”

A short, skinny man with unusually bright-red hair came out from behind the curtains. “Yes, master?”

“Did you hear everything they said while I was out of the room?”

"Yes, master. Their discussion was very unusual, though. Their real names are not Anna and David, they are Abi and Chris. Besides some strange words about a potter named Harry, they seemed to think they are from another world and came to Meynch through a gate or a portal of some sort."

Micah's eyes widened, and he muttered, "I knew they were lying. I knew there was something different about them." Then he turned to Rogan. "I have an errand for you. Go to the courthouse and ask for Judge Faln…"

❧ ❧ ❧ ❧

"This is far enough. I'm opening the scroll." Chris said as he and his sister walked by the side of the road.

"No, don't!" Abi grabbed his hand as he was about to unfold it. "What if it's a confidental message? Maybe Micah was being secretive for a reason. If it's really that important, we could be getting ourselves into huge trouble simply by knowing what it is. More than anything, we need to stay out of everyone's way until we can find a way home."

"If it's so dangerous, why would he give it to us? We're just a couple of kids."

"Maybe he thinks no one will suspect us to be messengers. I don't know, but are you willing to take the risk that I'm right?"

Chris nodded slowly. "All right. I see your point. But let's at least see if anyone can answer our question better than Micah did and maybe give us some more information about this place. I'm betting any random person off the street will be much more cooperative than Micah was." Chris turned to a pretty, young blonde who was raking the leaves in the front yard of one of the houses. "Excuse me, miss, but would you happen to know who the Stranger is?"

The girl looked up in surprise. She gazed at them for a moment, and then made a motion for them to come inside.

Chris looked at Abi, shrugged, and went inside after the girl. Abi looked around cautiously but soon followed.

After closing and locking the door, the girl spoke to Chris, ignoring Abi. "It's dangerous to speak about anything to do with him in public. The lawmen made a rule after he died, saying the only people that are allowed to talk about the Stranger are them." She leaned close to Chris, her breath tickling his cheek. "And they enforce it."

"So do you know where he is now?" Chris asked, more than a little irritation in his voice. Usually he welcomed girls' attention, and even encouraged it, but right now he just wanted to get back home where everything was normal, where he could do whatever he wanted and forget this whole thing ever happened. This girl's flirting only wasted time, and he was getting impatient. He stepped back.

She sighed and shook her head, her blond curls bouncing. "He's dead. Where else would he be but six feet under? The only time I saw him was three weeks before the lawmen killed him."

"And just why do you think that will help us?" Abi asked impatiently. She had noticed the girl's flirtatious attitude toward her brother, and though she was used to girls who found her brother attractive, this particular girl seemed to be flirting with him to hide something. Abi had a feeling the girl would have acted the same way to anyone asking the questions Chris was, just so she could distract them. *Why am I not surprised? Everyone in this town we've met so far has been hiding something*, Abi thought.

"Hey, if you don't want to know, you can go." The girl pouted prettily.

When there was no comment, she batted her eyelashes at Chris and started her story. "He came to me in a side alley by the Courtyard of the Virgins and told me to repent of my sins. 'Well,' I said, 'I don't consider myself sinful.'

"'Yet you are,' and he proceeded to tell me all the things I had done to break the law of the King that day. Naturally, I told him he was accusing me unfairly, that he had no right to judge me, and I walked away.

"But as I left, a lawmen stepped in front of me, asking where the man I was talking with went. I pointed behind me. He stared at me like I was from another dimension." Abi started at that, but the girl didn't notice, "'Lass, there is no one behind you,' he said. I turned around, expecting to see the man walking away. But nobody was there! The only way he could have gone out of the alley was if he had walked around me and the lawmen. But he had simply disappeared. That's when I knew he was the Stranger everyone's been talking about.

"Ever since, I've helped the friends of the Stranger spread his teachings."

"And the reason would be…," Abi questioned.

The girl finally noticed Abi, looking her over. *I wonder if she thinks I'm his girlfriend, like Kes did.* The thought made Abi smirk. "Why? Because I believe what he says, of course. Why else?" Seeing Abi's obvious doubt, she continued, "Just between us," the young woman leaned close to Abi, "one of the Stranger's followers is *so* cute! I've been trying to get him to notice me forever, and this is a perfect opprotunity."

Abi raised her eyebrows. "So you put your life in danger by supporting an illegal group because a cute guy is in it? I guessed."

The atmosphere between them was tense until Chris intervened. "So…where exactly is this Courtyard of the Virgins?"

She broke her icy stare at Abi and blinked, seeming to recover her composure, then turned and looked coyly at Chris. "Oh, you can't go in. It's only for unmarried girls. All women can come to draw fresh water from the well, but it's specifically a place where we can gather without the interference of fathers or husbands. Most use it simply to catch up on the local gossip, but a girl also goes there right before she gets married for a…goodbye ceremony, of sorts."

"Like a bachelorette party," Abi whispered to her brother. "You probably don't want to go in there."

Chris's face reddened up to the tips of his ears. "I—I knew that from the name, obviously," he stammered. "Anna," Chris motioned to Abi, "can go in."

"Anna. What a…quaint name," the girl's lip curled ever so slightly. "What's *your* name?" she asked Chris.

"David," Chris replied, then began to smoothly recite a short, impromptu history since it was apparent the girl didn't recognize them. "Our parents moved us away for a while, but we've come back to visit family."

"I see," she said slowly as if she was not fully convinced. "Would you like to stay for dinner?"

Chris was about to say something, but Abi interrupted. "I'm sorry, but we really must go. We don't want to be late for our…" Abi looked askance at Chris, "…visit with our family. They're probably waiting for us right now."

"All right," the girl said frostily, "If that is your wish."

As they were leaving, Chris turned around. "Oh, you never told us your name."

"Oh, silly me. How will you be able to find me so we can…*talk* again," she fluttered her eyelashes at Chris and smiled, "without knowing my name? My name is Pliandra."

Betrayed

Abi's eyes widened. She opened her mouth to speak, but Chris quickly slapped his hand over her mouth, muffling her words. "We really must be going. Bye," he said and went out the door, dragging Abi behind him.

Once a distance away from the house, Chris ducked into a side alley and took his hand off Abi's mouth. The setting sun colored the sky with vibrant hues of pink and violet, but neither of them noticed.

"Abi!" Chris was about to lecture her, but she interrupted.

"We have a problem. Didn't Kes say Pliandra was, like, the gossip queen? I bet that in less than ten seconds everyone will know we're here! I am *so* glad we did not tell her our real reason for being here. But people might look to see if there is anyone who is related to an Anna and David, and there won't be! Then everyone will know we're strangers, the lawmen will kill us, and we'll never see Earth again!"

"Abi, calm down."

Abi paused.

"Now," Chris said quietly, "breathe."

Abi inhaled deeply, and exhaled slowly. "All right," she said. "I'm calm."

"Good. Now, the only thing we can do is try to find the Stranger before the lawmen people find *us*."

"You're forgetting something," a voice behind them commented dryly.

Abi and Chris whirled around to find an old man staring at them and smiling slightly. He continued, "Children, your plan is admirable, easy, and to the point. But maybe you haven't noticed that you're outnumbered roughly one to ten *thousand*."

"What do you mean? There can't be that many lawmen. I mean, most of the people we've met are either peasants or merchants."

"There are a majority of peasants and merchants but not by a huge amount. Out of the sixty or seventy thousand people, the majority are obviously peasants and merchants, or else our economy would flounder. But the lawmen don't need to be the majority; they are powerful enough to have their eyes and ears everywhere."

"I see," Chris said. "It's like Hitler and the Nazis," he explained to Abi, who still looked vaguely confused. "The Nazis were a minority in Germany, so many people just ignored them. But all the while, Hitler was gaining power and influence until he was easily elected chancellor. Weren't you listening in history class, or did you zone out then too?"

"Like you're one to talk. You're too busy flirting with anything in a skirt to even notice there is a teacher in the room!"

The older man interrupted their budding argument. "You are sadly mistaken if you think that you can just ignore the lawmen and they will go away. They have power and influence, like this Hitler of yours, and they will find you."

Chris was about to say something, but suddenly his expression changed. He felt the same urge to hide the truth as he had felt with Micah. "Who are you, anyway? How do we know we can trust you?"

Abi heard footsteps behind them just as the old man replied.

"You don't."

The last thing Chris saw was the man's evil grin.

"Where am I?" Chris's head ached but with effort. Then he opened his eyes.

"In some sort of jail," Abi replied from behind him. "You got quite a knock on the head. Not hard enough to create a knot, but you'll probably be black and blue for a while."

"Abi…" Chris started to turn around, but his headache intensified to new heights. "My head hurts. Can you come where I can see you?"

Abi stood up and walked over to sit next to Chris. "Does this help?"

"Yeah. Thanks. So…why exactly are we here?"

"I don't know," Abi replied.

For a long time, they were silent. Chris looked around the jail cell for potential escape routes. There was one small window and the door, but they were both blocked by steel bars. Then a man, probably the jailer, came up to the door. He was very young, maybe only a few years older than Chris. He was heavily built, with a round stomach and broad shoulders, and his face was pinched and wrinkled.

"Excuse me, but could you please tell us why we're here?" Chris called out, going for the we're-just-innocent-kids-who-aren't-capable-of-illegal-activity approach. "We didn't do anything wrong."

"Apparently, you did. Judge Faln got a call from the head prosecutor, Micah…"

"Wait, did you say Micah?" Abi asked.

"Yes. Why do you ask? Do you recognize the name?" the young man said suspiciously.

"No, it's just…" Abi searched her mind for something she could say that was at least a little true. "One of my friends has a crush on a guy named Micah."

He looked at her curiously then continued. "Well, Micah said that you were looking for the Stranger, and so Judge Faln immediately sent his advisor, Najd and ten lawmen went out to find you, but they were unsuccessful until they heard the latest bit of gossip. Apparently you went to Pliandra, which, by the way, if you were trying to avoid being caught, wasn't a very wise move because whatever anyone tells Pliandra, she tells us immediately."

"We know," Abi said, glaring at Chris.

"Hey, don't blame me!" Chris said. "She was hot, but by the time she opened her mouth, I knew she was a little weird."

"They heard you were going to head for the Courtyard of the Virgins, and so they set out to intercept you. Najd went into a side alley, claimed he heard you saying illegal things, and brought you here. When the lawmen searched you, they found a scroll with Micah's seal that said you were criminals."

“We’re doomed,” Chris said simply.

“Why do you say that? Is it because you finally recognize your guilt?” the jailer asked.

“No. We’re doomed because we made the stupid decision to trust those people you mentioned, and now we find out they all betrayed us.”

The "Great" Escape

"When you say it like that, it makes you sound like the victims," the jailer said quietly.

"We are," Abi retorted. "Do we really look like hardened criminals?"

The jailer was about to respond when a voice called, "Peter! The judge needs you right away."

"Yes, sir," Peter said. With a regretful glance at Abi and Chris, he turned and walked away.

"I can't believe Micah's a lawman!" Abi exclaimed after he had left.

"I can't, either. He acted like he really wanted to help us. Although, his eyes were a little freaky, and his story of the Stranger did defend the lawmen."

"I guess you were right, Chris," Abi said grudgingly. "We should have opened that scroll."

Chris donned a mask of complete shock. "Excuse me? What was that you said?"

"Ugh, stop being annoying. You were right and I was wrong. Back to the problem at hand."

"Can I just say 'I told you so?'" Chris had a self-satisfied smirk plastered on his face. "And, since I was the one who wanted to do the mature thing instead of being naïve, I will remind you of this moment later, when you say that I need to grow up."

"Whatever. Anyway, the old man being a lawman wasn't that much of a surprise. He knew how many lawmen there were and everything, and when I heard the footsteps of the other lawmen, that really cinched it for me. Of course, I didn't know then that there were other lawmen hiding during the conversation. But now we have to focus on getting out of here. Have any ideas?"

"Actually, I was just thinking of one…"

The next day, the jailer returned. "It looks like you are going to be on trial tomorrow."

He found Chris asleep at one end of the cell and Abi leaning on the wall at the other.

"Hello again. Your name is Peter, right?" Abi stood up slowly, stretching her arms to relieve the soreness that came from sleeping on a hard cell floor. *Time for action.* She untied her hair and brushed it out with her fingers, looking at the jailer from the corner of her eye.

"Uh, yeah." Peter looked a little dazed.

She concealed a smile. Chris's plan might just work. *Just act all girly and pretty and sweet and stuff, and you'll have him wrapped around your little finger*, he had said. His plan was a little embarrassing and rather manipulative, but after a whole night in that pitch-black cell with rats and other nasty creatures, she was willing to do just about anything to escape.

"By the way, I'm thinking of ditching him," Abi said, motioning to Chris. "He's been a real pain, landing us here in jail. I think I like you better." Abi batted her eyelashes at Peter like Pliandra had done to Chris the other day, hoping she did not look like an idiot who had something stuck in her eye. He came so close to the bars that Abi could touch him, and she pulled his arm toward her, turning his back to Chris. As Chris opened his eyes and crawled behind Peter, reaching through the bars to snatch his keys from his belt, Abi flashed a dazzling smile. "You are so…gullible."

Peter started at that, felt the keys hit his head, and fell down.

"Wow, you are good," Chris said as he unlocked the door. "I didn't know you even had it in you. You really had the poor guy on the hook."

"I feel bad, though," Abi replied. "The guy seemed pretty nice, even though he was working for the lawmen." She looked at Chris, sure her face was flaming in embarrassment from the question she was about to ask. "Do you really think I'm pretty?"

"Well, let me put it this way. That was positive affirmation. If I hadn't said that, would you have still done it?"

"No, but…hey! So you *don't* think I'm pretty? Really?" *I mean, I knew I wasn't that attractive, but to get it from my own brother—*

Chris avoided her gaze. "Well…" When Abi glared at him fiercely, he laughed. "Kidding! Anyway, like they say, 'all is fair in love and war.' Besides, it's not like we killed him. He'll wake up soon enough perfectly unharmed, except for a throbbing headache. By then, we'll be long gone, hopefully. Trust me, lots of guys here feel no shame about flirting with *you*, including a certain guy. Does the name *Nathan* ring a bell?" Abi blushed as Chris got the door open, and he and Abi walked out.

He thinks I didn't notice that he never answered my question. I guess he can't bring himself to lie to me. Wow, I never thought that would hurt so much…

"Wait just a minute!" a voice said from behind them. They turned to see Peter struggling to his feet, rubbing his head, but looking more angry than injured. "Did you really think it would be that easy to overpower me? That the lawmen would really place an incompetent boy to guard the dangerous strangers?"

"Wait a second." Chris held up his hands, swaying slightly and shutting his eyes as if in deep concentration. "I'm sensing some deep-seated insecurity here," Chris said in an insincere, comforting voice. "Has someone called you this before?"

"Shut up! Just get back in the cell, and no one will get hurt."

Chris pulled Abi's arm, telling her to run, but Peter quickly yanked out a wicked-looking broadsword and held it in front of him with both hands. "Don't even think about it."

I don't know how to fight! We're dead!

Chris met Abi's frantic gaze for a split second and seemed to read her thoughts.

Pushing her behind him and against the far wall, he jumped on Peter, deftly avoiding the sharp point of the sword, and grabbed him in a wrestling headlock. Peter tried to flip him off, but Chris held on tenaciously.

Peter's meaty fist flew up and met Chris' jaw straight on, but Chris just grunted.

Abi looked on helplessly. *I have to do something!* She scanned the prison and saw a chair in the corner, probably for the guard. She ran to it, picked it up, and banged Peter on the head repeatedly. "Let—my—brother—go!"

Chris, his face now taking on a purplish tinge with newly forming bruises, let go of Peter's head for a quick second and landed a solid kick into his midsection. Peter bent over, clutching his stomach, and Abi smashed him over the head with the chair as hard as she could.

With a groan, he went down, his eyes fluttering shut.

Looking at her brother, Abi laughed. "I will never complain about you being a jock again."

Chris tried to smile, but his cut lip made him wince.

Abi and Chris walked up a dark spiral stairway, tense and alert in case of any more encounters with guards, and at the end they saw another door that was rimmed in light. Chris opened it to find him and Abi in the bustling city of Meynch again.

They walked through the side streets so intent on avoiding any lawmen that they didn't see the curious stares and hear the whispers among a group of women in the market.

"Who are those kids?" one lady asked.

"I think they are supposed to be on trial tomorrow," another responded.

"They must have escaped from the jail."

"I wonder if the judge knows. Someone should tell him."

"Why should we? After all, the judge is a tyrant. Who knows what he'll do to the kids. Personally, if we don't tell, that's two more children who don't have to be censored for the rest of their lives," another lady said as she joined the cluster of women.

"Shhh, Marla! It's dangerous to voice such an opinion out loud."

"I heard before you didn't want to get involved with anyone associated with the lawmen. What changed your mind?"

"Those children," Marla replied simply. "They changed my mind."

❧ ❧ ❧ ❧

Abi and Chris were only a few feet away from the archway through which they had entered Meynch when they heard a voice behind them. "Hello again, children."

They whirled around, but the speaker was hidden in the shadows of an alley. "Who are you? What do you want?" Chris said suspiciously.

The person stepped forward into the light. "You don't remember Marla, wife of Kesan?" she asked.

Abi's mouth dropped open. *She hated us! She wanted us out of her house as soon as possible! Why would she seek us out?*

"Yes," Chris said quietly. "Yes, we do."

Reunion

"Come with me. It's not safe here." Marla led them away from the open street into the side alley she had come out from.

"You didn't even want us to stay at your house because you were so afraid of the lawmen. What made you change your mind?" Abi asked, her tone far from trusting.

"After you left, my husband and I had a long talk. You see, I didn't know that Kes was a friend of the Stranger. My husband had been studying the Stranger's teachings for a while now, but I thought his interest was mere curiosity. When he finally told me, I was very angry with him for keeping something that important from me, especially since the lawmen are even now fervent in their desire to arrest and kill any followers of the Stranger. But as he explained your…situation to me, I understood how he felt obligated to help you, yet I still discouraged him from bringing you back. It was just too dangerous to us and our family.

"But when he heard you had been captured by the lawmen, he felt extremely guilty about letting you go into danger, so I resolved to find you and bring you back. I was planning a jailbreak, but apparently you managed that yourselves. How did you do it? The prison is high-security clearance. You can't even get one foot away from the cells without a guard asking you for the appropriate papers stating that you are not a prisoner."

"What guards?" Chris asked. "The only guard we saw was the jailer, and he wasn't harsh at all. A little hard to take down, but we managed well enough." Chris looked at his sister. "Remind me never to underestimate you again. You were vicious." He grinned at her embarrassment.

"Well, young man, your face says otherwise," Marla said. "We need to get you cleaned up. People won't even need to recognize you as strangers, because your face looks like you just escaped from jail."

"Anyway," Chris said, trying to change the subject, "from what I understand about the system here, harboring us would make you just as guilty in their eyes. Are you sure you want to let us stay at your house?"

"Whether or not I'm sure, I am obligated to help you," Marla said. "You will understand soon enough."

Sometime later, they arrived at Kes's house. It was a modest cottage that was almost hidden by the enormous oak trees that surrounded it. Just like in Abi's first vision, they had passed the landmark of a house with a blue roof, and a stone marker calling it the Area of Merchants. It was at least a mile away from the main part of Meynch, Marla had said as they walked, though still considered part of the town. Marla went in first.

"Kes, I brought the kids," she called out. "He's upstairs resting," she said to Abi and Chris.

A voice from above boomed, "Our kids are right here!"

"No, *the* kids, remember?"

"Oh!" Abi and Chris heard a loud thump, and then Kes came down the stairs. He stood in front of them and clasped his hands in front of him, looking very embarrassed. "I suppose my wife explained the whole story to you. I should never have let you go without taking precautions so you would be safe. I'm sorry. But you can stay with us until we figure out how to get you back home…somehow."

"Thank you," Chris said. Not long ago, he would have taken Kes's words at face value and just gone with the flow, but getting beat up had a way of putting things in perspective for him. He needed to watch out for himself and his sister now, and he wanted to trust Kes, but…*why were they "obligated" to help us?*

"Here, let me show you where you will sleep." Kes led them up the stairs to a row of doors. He opened one of them and said, "Nathan!"

Nathan came out of the room and replied, "Yes, Father?"

"This young lad…what's your name?"

Chris decided to be honest, just in case he or Abi slipped by accident. It was not as if Meynch had any record of them or important information anyway. But he kept his mental guard up. "My real name is Chris, but I told Pliandra that my name was David."

"A wise idea," Kes said. "Chris will stay with you."

"Yes, Father." Nathan let Chris go in first, but right before Nathan himself went in, he winked at Abi. "Have fun," he whispered and disappeared inside.

"As for you…what's your name, lass?"

Abi followed Chris's lead. "Chris told Pliandra my name was Anna, but my real name is Abigale. You can call me Abi."

"Abi, you will stay with Weana. And while you're here, I'd appreciate it if you'd help my wife look after her." Kes pointed to a room next to Nathan's.

"Of course," Abi said, now a little worried. *Wow, really? Did Marla help us just so I could babysit their kid? Is that her "obligation?"*

She had babysat their neighbor's five-year-old boy last year, and she now regretted it as one of the worst decisions of her life so far. The boy had broken everything that could be broken and yelled the whole time. *Oh, well, you can't look a gift horse in the mouth. I suppose I should be glad she helped us at all. Hopefully girls are more well-mannered, right?* Abi thought to herself as she opened the door to go inside.

She found Weana sleeping peacefully in her bed. *Whew!* Abi thought and went to the bed nearby to take a nap herself. On the bed were three pairs of jeans, two dark and one faded, and two dresses, probably for her to wear while she was there. She hung them up in the closet beside her bed, combed her hair with the brush on the dresser, braided it, took off her shoes, and snuggled under the sheets. She closed her eyes, intending just to relax for a moment, but the irresistible call of undisturbed slumber beckoned to her…

She drifted through the house like a ghost. She first saw her parents' room. Her mom was the only one there. *Where's Dad?* Abi wondered. Then she went in her room. Everything was just as she had left it. *The bed hasn't even been made,* Abi thought, more than a little puzzled. *Usually Dad's nice enough to make my bed if I forget.* Then she happened to glance at the time on her digital clock. *Eight forty a.m.!*

Kes's House

Abi woke up suddenly. *Wait, so it's only been ten minutes back home? It's been hours here! We could spend days here, and our parents wouldn't even notice!* She sighed. *Well, I guess that's not too bad because it keeps Mom and Dad from freaking out for a while. At least until we get back.* She yawned. *I've never felt so tired this early in the day... maybe traveling to another dimension saps your energy somehow.* Her eyes drifted closed, and soon she was sleeping peacefully.

Meanwhile, Chris was getting a tour of Nathan's spacious room.

"So what's in there?" Chris pointed to a large trunk. "Your diary?"

Nathan grinned but didn't open it. "Nope. That has all the certificates and awards that I got when I studied law."

"You what?"

"Every child over six years old has to study the law of the King for six years, and then they are given the choice to study further to become a lawman or pursue a different path."

"We have something kind of like that back home. It's called grade school. But we're not allowed to quit after six years. We have to go to elementary school, middle school, and high school for twelve years. Wait, you said you study to be a lawman?"

"Yeah, we have to. That was mandated by the King himself. Actually, the fact that we get a chance to study the law for ourselves is a good thing because it gives us a better understanding of the laws, and it's harder for the lawmen to deceive us when they try to twist the law to serve their own purposes."

"Wow. So how many certificates *have* you gotten?"

"About fifty…"

"Really?" Chris began to look at Nathan in a new light.

"…minus forty-nine." He opened the drawer, letting Chris see one small sheet of paper.

"So, one."

"What, you can't subtract now?"

Chris laughed. "You seem like a pretty chill guy. I give you permission to crush on my sister."

"What?" Nathan's eyes widened.

Chris smirked. "Where am I sleeping?"

"Over here," Nathan said, trying to quickly recover from his embarrassment. He led Chris to a large bed at one side of the room. "I sleep over here." Nathan pointed to another bed on the other side of the room.

"Hey, how come you get the bigger bed? Don't you know, you always give the biggest bed to the," Chris pointed to himself with both hands, "guest of honor?"

"I don't see any honored guest here, do you?" Nathan pretended to look around the room. "But I do see a fugitive with a not-so-pretty face."

"It's all right. You're too stuck on my sister to see my amazing looks. But she didn't get all the pretty genes. Even banged up, I'm a male model." Chris struck a exaggerated pose.

Nathan cocked his head to the side, studying Chris, then grinned. "Nope, I still think your sister's prettier."

"Hey, if I were you, I would be trying to get on my good side, or else you won't get within fifty feet of said sister."

Nathan was about to retort, when Marla's voice called from downstairs. "Nathan!"

"Yes?" Nathan opened the door wider.

"Can you go to the market and pick up some bread?"

"Okay," Nathan said as he went downstairs to go outside.

"And, Nathan?"

"Yes?" Nathan asked, dragging the word out a bit longer this time.

"Don't tell anyone Chris and Abigale, I mean David and Anna, are staying with us, all right?"

"Yes, I'm going to tell the whole world that we have two fugitives staying at our house." Nathan said sarcastically.

"What was that?"

"Never mind. I won't. I'll be careful."

With that Nathan disappeared out the door.

Chris sat down on his bed and yawned. His eyelids felt heavy, and his body sagged. *I don't know why I'm so tired all of a sudden. Maybe I'll just take a quick nap…*

His eyes closed, and he fell back against the bed.

About a half-hour later, Marla looked in her food pantry. "Oops." She went upstairs into Abi's room.

"Abigale!"

"Yes, madam?" Abi came out of her room.

"Do you know where my husband is? I just sent Nathan to the market, and I forgot to tell him to get firewood on the way back."

"I'm not sure, but I can go tell Nathan, if you want."

"Oh, no, I wouldn't want to put you through any trouble. You're our guest."

"No, really, it's the least I can do," Abi assured. "I'll be fine."

"But you are a wanted fugitive. It's not a good idea to go out on your own. Can you get your brother to go with you?"

Abi laughed. "Chris is sleeping like a baby and snoring like a pig. I couldn't wake him up even if I tried. Really, it's okay. I can make it," Abi said.

"Are you sure? Because I can wait for Kes—"

"No, it's fine. I'll just stay out of sight."

Marla still looked unsure. "The market is not far, and it should be crowded enough that you can just slip in and out without anyone noticing you. If you can't find him, or if someone spots you, just come back. Don't stay around there. Are you really sure about this? I would never forgive myself if I got you recaptured."

"Don't worry, I'll be fine. Like I said, it's the least I can do since you took in me and my brother. Firewood is pretty important, right?" Abi said.

Marla smiled. "Yes, it is, at least here. Thank you. Be careful. Stay out of sight."

When Abi went back inside her room to put on her shoes, she thought of something. *Oh, gosh, what if Nathan tries to talk to me? I'm not one of those flirty, put-themselves-out-there girls. I'll probably make a fool of myself trying to impress him.*

Ugh, get a hold of yourself! Abi gave herself a mental shake. *I need to stay focused. Go in, tell Nathan, get out. I've talked to him, what, like once so far? Not exactly a solid foundation for a relationship. And besides, even if I actually was pretty and confident and could get him to like me, a relationship with a guy in another dimension is totally awkward. As if a long distance relationship isn't hard enough, it's like a long distance relationship* plus *the barriers of time and space.*

Shocking News

Marla had given her some money—which was surprisingly like American dollar bills, except it was white, and where the face of a president was supposed to be, there was a picture of a crown and a shepherd's staff—and she sent her on her way. But Abi had already gone a mile away from the house when she realized she had forgotten to ask how to get to the market.

Abi paused. *I could go back. But that would take way too long. The only other option is to ask someone in the town for directions, and that would show that I am a stranger because probably everyone in the town knows where the market is. Plus it would get me some unwanted attention. And then the lawmen will find us again.*

I guess I'm going to have to risk it though. Lucky for me, Marla said Meynch is huge. Even though the lawmen have "eyes and ears everywhere," the odds of running into the same people twice should be pretty slim.

Once she got to the town, she asked the first person she saw, an old lady, if she knew where the market was. The lady looked at her curiously for a moment and then gave her detailed directions in the condescending voice one would use for a little child. It irritated Abi to no end, but she wisely kept her mouth shut and graciously thanked the older woman.

After she followed the lady's directions and found the market, she was reminded of a picture she had seen in her history textbook of a marketplace in Europe during the Dark Ages. It was made up of stands like the one put up for lemonade, but they were covered by tarps. The stands lined either side of the street for several blocks. The merchants behind each one sold everything imaginable, from fruits and vegetables to clothes to books. She walked through it, trying to blend in and at the same time look for Nathan.

After a while, she saw someone who looked like him and was about to call out to him when an all-too-familiar male voice asked, "Why are you out on the streets alone, child?"

The man grasped her arm and turned her around to face him, and Abi stared at him, shocked.

"Dad!"

"Is that you, Abi?" He raised both his eyebrows—the gesture he reserved for when he was completely shocked.

Abi was so shocked to see her dad here in Meynch that she couldn't seem to do anything but stare blankly at her father. She finally managed out a "Yeah."

"Why are you here?"

Abi blinked her eyes to recover and then quickly poured out the whole story, starting from first seeing the gate, leaving out only the specifics of how she escaped from prison. She hesitated, but told her father about her weird dreams/visions of Meynch. Her father murmured an occasional, "uh huh," "hmm," or "oh."

After she finished, her father commented dryly, "So I'm assuming you and Chris *don't* know why you're here."

Abi felt the intense urge to hug her father, but she pushed it down. She needed some answers first. "Dad, what are *you* doing here?"

"I don't know why I was sent back here, either."

"Oh well, so now that you've come, that means you can help us figure out how we can all go home—wait, did you say *back* here?"

Her father sighed. "I knew I would have to tell you children some day, but I didn't imagine it would be under such circumstances."

"Tell us what?" Abi said almost angrily.

"I don't know how to put this." Mr. Candial sighed again, deeper this time, and ran his hand through his hair. "You…I am not from Earth. What I mean is, we—you and Chris and I—were born here. In Meynch."

Secrets Revealed

"We *what*!" Abi yelled so loudly that the other people in the market turned their heads.

"Abi, keep your voice down," her father reprimanded. "You're a stranger, remember? According to your story, that's equivalent to being on FBI's most wanted list. You don't want to draw attention to yourself."

Abi blushed, but refused to back down. "Don't change the subject! When were you going to get around to telling us this?" Abi said quieter than before but still angry.

"Well, I…"

"*When?*"

"Don't you use that tone with me, young lady. I didn't think it was necessary to burden a kid your age with the knowledge that you're not just from a different country, you're from another dimension!" Mr. Candial turned red, and a tic between his eyebrows twitched—a telltale spasm that showed he was nervous. "Anyway, it doesn't change anything."

"Are you *kidding*? It changes *everything*! The only reason the lawmen tossed us in prison is because we're strangers, and if we were born here, then we're not even strangers at all! We don't have to hide from them!"

Her father looked away. "We *are* strangers here," he said quietly.

"What? But you just said…"

"I'll explain at Kes's house," her father said while still not looking at her.

"Dad, if there are any more secrets, please just tell me," Abi asked pleadingly.

"Chris has to know, as well."

"Right. Chris." Abi realized her dad was using Chris as an excuse not to tell her now, but she decided not to press her point. He was already feeling the weight of his secrets.

"Let's go," and Dad led her back to Kes's house.

As they neared Kes's cottage, her father sighed, and Abi looked at him curiously. His eyes held a wistful gleam as if he was reminded of some fond memory.

Abi opened her mouth to confront him, but he knocked on the door of the home, avoiding Abi's gaze. Kes answered the door immediately.

"Abi! Marla was just looking for you. You took so long that she was worried you had ran into some trouble at the market."

"I'm sorry. I didn't mean to worry her." Abi deliberately did not introduce her father to Kes, wanting to see how they would greet each other.

Kes stared intently at Mr. Candial but spoke to Abi. "Who is this man?" he asked in a voice that said little but implied much.

"Hello, Kes. Abi has told me all about you," Abi's father said.

Abi was not blind to the flash of recognition and surprise on Kes's face and the unspoken communication that passed between her father and Kes. Kes led them to a couch in one of the spacious rooms, and there was a long, awkward silence in which Abi did some serious thinking.

This is so frustrating! It's obvious Dad knows Kes and that neither of them want me to know that they know each other. What are they trying to hide? Abi thought back to the way Kes had accepted their being from another world with relative ease, and she remembered that even when they had first met him, Abi noticed that Kes looked a lot like her dad. Marla had said she felt "obligated" to help them. And now Abi could see the casual, almost intimate way Kes treated her dad and vice versa, as if their relationship was deep and long-lasting. There was some sort of connection between all these facts.

But the only one that came to mind was ridiculous, wasn't it? Yet there was no other reasonable conclusion.

Abi could not take the uncomfortable silence anymore, and her question finally burst out.

"Are you guys related?"

Kes and her dad slowly turned to look at her. "Why would you think that?" Kes asked in a neutral voice.

His voice was so nonchalant, in fact, that for a moment Abi doubted her reasoning. In that moment, Kes gave Abi's father a look that said, *Apparently you haven't told them yet. Why?*

Dad looked away and clenched his jaw.

"It's the only explanation that makes sense. He told me he was born here. You act like you know each other well, but you look too much alike to be just friends," Abi finally said, and they looked at her again.

"Abi, you have been introduced to Kes," Dad said, "but probably not with full honesty." He let out a long breath as if his next words pained him. "Abi, meet my twin, Kes."

"Your *what!*" Abi stood up. "But you guys don't look *that* much alike!"

"I believe the term for us is *fraternal* twins," Kes responded.

"You've got to be kidding me!" *Just when I was starting to think I solved all the mysteries in Meynch, here comes another secret to change my life!* Abi was beginning to be overwhelmed. "So not only is my dad from another world, not only am I half-alien or whatever you people are, but I have family that I've never heard of in another dimension!" She laughed with more than a tinge of hysteria. "I mean, get a load of this! I can't wait to draw my family tree. 'Oh, yeah, half my family lives in another dimension.' That'll go over well."

"Abi, calm down," her father said. "I'm sorry this is coming at you all at once, but you need to get a hold of yourself."

"Calm down? Get a hold of myself? Are you *kidding* me? How did you expect me to react to this, Dad? Did you think I would be completely nonchalant about finding out I'm *half-alien*?"

"Stop calling yourself that!" Dad said sternly. "The people of Meynch are no more alien than you or I."

Abi's anger partially dissolved at the hurt look on her father's face, and her eyes welled with tears. "Then what am I, Dad?" she asked softly. "What are we?"

"Hey, Abi," a voice interrupted. They all looked up to Chris who was coming down the stairs, rubbing his eyes. "I dreamt this really weird dream—" He stopped mid-sentence when he saw the man beside his sister. "Dad?"

"Yes, Chris, " Abi said, and Chris looked at her. She was clearly very upset at the man next to her. "It's Dad."

"What—who—what are you *doing* here!"

"It's a long story," Abi and her father said at the same time, and she frowned at him.

"Come sit down," Dad said. "It's time to tell you everything."

Mr. Candial's Past

Abi crossed her arms and leaned back against the couch; her face was a hard, unresponsive mask. Chris was little better as he struggled to understand what was going on.

In spite of his children's hostility, Mr. Candial told his story clearly and honestly, trying to make up for the years of half truths and secrets.

"Let me start by explaining that since Meynch is such a closely-knit town, when children are born in Meynch, it is a very big event. There is a celebration for every newborn, and the parents are showered with advice and gifts from friends and family.

"I was born in Meynch at the time when the lawmen sincerely sought to help their fellow man and follow the laws of the land. But Kes's and my birth, I am told, was a strange event.

"There was a prophetess that used to live on the mountain—a reclusive, old lady whom no one of our generation had ever seen. It was rumored that many years ago she had been one of the most beloved people in Meynch, —a kindly, wise woman whom many would go to for counsel. But seeking a higher wisdom than her own, she had traveled the difficult road to the King's castle. The King, seeing her purity and honesty, had given her a rare honor. He had invited her to live in the castle and serve him instead of returning to Meynch. Though she was greatly tempted by a life of ease and comfort, she declined his offer because she preferred to serve the people of Meynch closer to the valley as she had done for most of her life. The King revealed to her that the proposal had been a test, and as a reward for her pure motives, the King gave her the incredible gift of foresight in addition to her natural wisdom. She chose to live in the mountain not far from Meynch, not in the center of town, so that people who sought her would now have to endure the rigorous test of character that was the journey up the mountain, although not to the extent that one would if they journeyed to the King's castle.

"Anyway, when I was born, she came down from the mountain for the first time in years, to the astonishment of the people of Meynch. She prophesied to my parents, saying my blood was not bonded to this world, that I was born to go to another land. She didn't say anything about Kes, though, and our parents thought that was strange since we were twins. But the people of Meynch took all her prophecies very seriously, and when they heard this, they told my parents to send me away when I came of age. My parents sadly sent me away on my thirteenth birthday, giving me enough food and supplies for four days.

"So I walked aimlessly for three days because nobody had told me where this other land was that I was supposed to go to. On the third day, I saw a man wearing a long, hooded jacket—an odd sight since it was the middle of summer—and leaning on a gold-leafed tree.

When he saw me, he stood up and smiled a welcoming and companionable smile as if he had known me all my life.

"'Welcome, Erroll,' he said. 'Did your parents name you before or after the prophetess came?'"

"I was not surprised he knew about the prophetess, for my parents had told me that the news of my unusual birth had spread to the entire town. 'Before, sir,' I replied.

"'Do you know what your name means?'"

"Before I could reply, he said, 'It means *wanderer*. You have been fulfilling your name these past few days. But your wandering has come to an end. Look.' And he pointed to the tree he had been leaning on.

"I looked at the trunk. It seemed to draw me closer until I was only an arm's length away. 'Drink this,' the man said, giving me a cup filled with a blood-red liquid. If it had been any other person giving me this, I would have been suspicious, but somehow I knew this man was trustworthy. I closed my eyes and drained the cup in one swallow. The taste of it was overwhelmingly bitter, and yet I was filled with the most wonderful feeling, as if I had been cleansed from the inside out. When I opened my eyes, I immediately knew something had changed. Everything looked different. I touched one of the golden leaves. This one was shaped differently than most leaves—in the shape of a lamb with a crown on its head. I pulled it off and, noticing that there was a groove in the tree shaped like the leaf, I pressed the leaf into it.

"Suddenly, the tree opened, and blazing, white light poured out of the hole. I stepped into it, not knowing what to expect. When I stepped out of the tree, I was in America.

"Of course, I was a fish out of water, and it took time and patience for me to adapt to my new environment. Needless to say, I was pretty socially awkward. The only thing I knew was who my new 'parents' were, and when I showed them the golden leaf, that was all I had to do. Someone had already told them what to do when I came, though I never found out who it was. Luckily, I eventually found your mother, a beautiful woman who was one of the rare few who saw my social ineptitude and loved me anyway. For almost twelve years, my life on earth was pretty uneventful.

"But one night, I had a very extraordinary dream. I won't go into the details, except to say that when I woke up, I knew I had to go back. So I went out in search of a way. After all those years, I had kept the golden leaf as a memento of my life before I came to earth. Soon I found a stone marker that had a hole shaped like my leaf, and beneath it was writing. It said, and I remember it clearly,

> Beware, O adventurous stranger,
>
> Before you stretch out your hand,
>
> Encounter you many a danger:
>
> The portal to another land.

"I remembered the place, told your mother (who was then pregnant with Chris) a vague excuse about going to visit my relatives, and that we would come back later that week. I put the leaf in the hole, held your mother tightly, and closed my eyes. The ground beneath us shook, and blazing light hurt my eyes, even though they were closed. When the shaking stopped, we opened our eyes in Meynch.

"Your mother didn't ask any questions about how we had gotten to Meynch. In fact, she seemed not to remember anything about the marker. She thanked me for introducing her to all my childhood friends and relatives and made herself a part of the community. It was a good thing, too, that we went when we did because the next day your mother went into labor. Chris was born, and three years later, Abi. The people accepted me and my family back into the town, and we lived happily for four years in Meynch, almost forgetting about earth. Almost.

"But we heard rumors about another person besides us stumbling onto the portal on earth and finding their way here. This man was extremely evil, and he took over the lawmen, causing their corruption. His fitting end was that another lawman murdered him, but one month later we had to flee for our lives. The people now hated anyone from another world because of what he had done, and they soon attempted to storm our house. We escaped back to earth safely, but we were determined never to return.

"The morning you left, I heard you wake up and followed you to make sure you weren't disobeying

Mom. When I saw you go through the gate, which was another portal, I went in after you. But the gate sent me to the middle of one of the forests beside the valley. Fortunately, I had played in the forest often as a kid. Unfortunately, I had forgotten how to navigate through it.

"So, as you can imagine, I got lost a lot, but eventually I found the town. I went to the market where I was sure I would meet you. And here I am."

Who Is the Stranger?

"So, Dad, basically for twelve years you thought it would be acceptable for you to hide that your children were not from the same world as the people they saw every day?" Chris voiced what everyone in the room, including Kes, was thinking.

Abi wanted to add her own angry exclamation, but something stopped her. Her father looked extremely contrite, and she felt a flash of pity for him. *Twelve years is a long time to keep such a huge secret*, she thought. *It must have been horrible for him to hide this for so long.*

Chris, on the other hand, thought back to his dad's brief version of the corruption of the lawmen. *Who was the man who took over? Why didn't Dad say who he was? Is it because he doesn't know, or is there another reason?*

"Hello, Mr. Erroll. I bet you've come back for your children, right?" Nathan said casually. Abi and Chris turned around to see Nathan walking inside, carrying a load of groceries in one hand and some firewood under his other arm.

"Oh, good, you got firewood." Marla took some of the bags and patted Nathan's head. "What a good, responsible boy. I didn't even have to remind you. I thought you had forgotten, so I sent Abi to tell you, but she met her father." She led Nathan to the kitchen.

"I'll make some coffee for the gentlemen and get some snacks for the kids," Marla said over her shoulder.

"She's a good wife," Dad said to Kes.

"Yes, I have been blessed." Kes smiled at his wife.

"Why is everyone so loud?" a small voice said from the stairs, and Weana came downstairs. "Hi, Papa and Uncle Scott," she said when she saw them on the couch. "Where's Nathan?"

"He's helping Mama in the kitchen." Kes took Weana's hand and said, "Let's go clean up your room. I saw some of your clothes stuffed under your bed yesterday, and you know I told you to hang them up," as he led her back to the stairs.

"Even Nathan and Weana know that we're related to them? Hello! Does no one see anything wrong with this picture?" Abi exclaimed incredulously. "Kes?" she called.

"Yes?" Kes answered from upstairs.

"When did you tell your kids about our family?"

"Oh, when she was about three or four. I didn't explain the whole 'other dimension' thing, since she was so young, but I wanted her to know that we had extended family just in case you showed up someday," Kes replied glibly, forgetting for a moment the presence of his twin brother. Fortunately, before he said anything else he would regret, he remembered and sheepishly grinned.

Abi looked at her father with a mixture of pain and anger, waiting for him to give an excuse about why he didn't tell them. Instead, he just held out his arms, and, even though she hesitated, her longing for comfort overcame her distrust. She went to him and snuggled close, letting the warmth of her daddy's embrace soothe her and putting aside her anger, though not completely. Chris allowed himself to be enfolded in his father's hug, as well.

"All I can say is, I'm sorry. I should have told you sooner, but I was a little ashamed of the trouble we brought to Meynch, and I was afraid that if I told you, you would find a way to go back and unknowingly bring more trouble." He held them tightly, and a tear slipped out of his eyes, but he quickly wiped it away. "I'm just glad you're safe, in spite of my blunders."

"Dad, we think the only way to get home is to find the Stranger," Chris said, loosening himself from his father's tight embrace. "We have a little information about him, but that was from a lawman."

"Micah, I know. Abi told me about what happened." Mr. Candial got a faraway look in his eyes. "We used to be childhood friends, Micah and I. And when I came back from Earth with your mom, we stayed with him for the first year because Kes had just gotten married, and we didn't want to disturb his time with his wife. But when the other man from Earth came, Micah changed for the worse. It was a gradual change, so gradual I didn't even notice until it was too late. He still let us stay in his house, but he was aloof and silent when before he had been fun-loving and played with you constantly. I almost wish we had never returned in the first place because our coming brought so much sorrow."

Chris saw that the atmosphere in the room was fast becoming depressing, and so he jumped up and said,

"Come on, guys! Yeah, so we've had some tough times and made some mistakes. So what? Put the past behind you and see the future before you." Chris paused and grinned. "Hey, that should be a famous quote!"

Abi smiled half-heartedly. "You're trying too hard," she said to her brother. *That's why Micah seemed familiar,* she thought. *He was with us here when we were kids.* She was still angry at her father for not telling them all of this before, but her main goal was to get home. Anger would only confuse and distract her from this purpose. She turned to her father. "So do you have any information about the Stranger?"

"No, I don't, because I was in a whole other world raising you guys. All I know is that he came two years after I left the second time."

"What? That's not possible! The timeline…it doesn't make sense at all!" Abi protested. She rubbed her head. "I'm trying to figure it out, and my head hurts."

Erroll placed a calming hand on his daughter's shoulder. "They *are* two different worlds," he said. "Doesn't it make sense that they would have two different ways to measure time?"

"Yeah, but…"

"We don't have time for buts," Chris said, interrupting the argument before it got any farther. He turned to Abi. "Remember back at Micah's cottage when you said that the only way to get home is to find the Stranger? You're right! What Dad said, what we've heard of the Stranger, it all fits!"

Abi looked at him skeptically. "I don't get it."

"Yes, it does! Think, Abigala!" Chris exclaimed, accidentally calling her by her full name in his enthusiasm. "Dad said before he came from this world to ours the first time, the man gave him a golden leaf *shaped like a lamb with a crown*! The Stranger died willingly, just like a lamb is sacrificed, but he claimed to be the *King's Son*!"

"Oh! I see!" Abi exclaimed. "The Stranger *is* the lamb with a crown! He was the one who led Dad to Earth!"

At the End of the Day

"But that still doesn't explain what our purpose is," Abi said after a moment's pause.

Chris shrugged. "Even my amazing deduction skills," he half-grinned, trying to lighten the mood again, "aren't that keen."

"Until you figure that out, we will be here to help," Kes said. He had quietly come down and sat down with them.

"Thank you, brother," Dad said, clasping his twin's hand.

Abi sat down beside her brother, putting a hand on his shoulder. "It's okay. We'll figure it out later. At least now, we have more people we can trust and are willing to help us."

Erroll looked out the window, noticing the sun quickly disappearing behind the horizon. "I agree, Abi. You'll figure it out in the morning."

"But, Dad!" Abi complained.

"No buts. You have a long day ahead of you, and you need your rest. Go to bed." Dad's tone invited no argument.

"All right, all right. Good night, Uncle Kes and Aunt Marla." Abi paused. "Can I call you that?"

"Sure," Kes replied, hugging Abi.

"Good night," Abi paused, "Nathan." She held out her hand for him to shake, but with a grin, he surprised her by bowing, taking her hand in his much larger one, and placing a respectful kiss upon it. "Good night, Abigale."

Abi raised a eyebrow at him and was surprised and flattered by the gallant motion but refrained from commenting. She did not want to ruin the moment. *But wait a second...if Kes is my uncle, and Nathan is Kes's son, then Nathan's my cousin! And he's flirting with me?! Eeew!* She snatched her hand from Nathan's grasp.

Nathan's smile did not falter. As if reading her mind, Nathan turned to Kes and said, "So did you forget to mention to Abi that I'm not your son?"

"Huh? You're not?" Abi blinked in shock. *I am* so *confused right now.*

Kes shook his head. "Nope. He's my apprentice. I love him like a son, though." With a mischievous twinkle in his eyes, he put a hand to his forehead and closed his eyes. "But alas, I'm stuck with an adorable little angel for a daughter." He winked at Weana, and she ran to his open arms.

"Silly Papa! I love you, too," Weana said into her father's neck as he lifted her up.

Everyone else smiled at the scene, but suddenly a loud snore came from behind them. Chris had apparently grown tired of waiting and was fast asleep on the couch.

"That's our cue." Nathan smirked at Chris's huddled form, turned to Abi, and extended his arm to her. "Shall we leave, m'lady?"

"We shall." She grinned and glanced back. "Farewell, all." She waved to her father as Nathan guided her upstairs.

"You're surprised, aren't you?" Nathan asked once they reached the bedrooms.

Abi glanced at him. She was still sorting out what had just happened. "I'm surprised about pretty much everything I've learned today. What's your point?"

"No, you thought I was your cousin, and when I…I mean…" he trailed off, his face flushing suddenly. "Never mind." He went inside his room and shut the door.

Abi looked after him, puzzled. "Boys." Her hopes lifted slightly, but she pushed them down. Pushing aside the strange encounter, she shrugged and went inside her own room.

When Weana came upstairs to sleep, she found Abi getting ready for bed. "Abi, my mama says you would read me my bedtime story." She looked at Abi pleadingly.

"Okay, Weana," she conceded, "I'll read you a story. Which one would you like?" Abi glanced at a small bookcase beside Weana's bed.

Weana went over to the shelf, grabbed a book with gold lining, and thrust it into Abi's hands.

"Read me this one," Weana commanded, getting into her bed and snuggling under the covers. Abi smiled, pulled the blankets up to Weana's chin, and sat at the end of Weana's bed, the mattress creaking loudly at the additional weight.

Abi smiled at the sweet sight the girl made with the covers pulled up to her chin. Opening the book, she read, "Once upon a time..."

When Abi finally finished reading the story, Weana was fast asleep. She got up from Weana's bed, tiptoed over to her own bed, and crept under her own warm comforter. She clasped her hands behind her head and looked up at the ceiling, her mind going back to the conversation with Nathan right before he went to bed.

Gosh, so much has happened today. Dad came to Meynch and told us that we were born here in another dimension, and so was he, which makes us...half-alien, or something. I don't know! It's so freaky that I can't even think about it. Oh, and by the way, we are now stuck in a different world until we find a guy everyone thinks is dead!

And as if that's not enough, Nathan is definitely acting like he's interested in me, and if he wasn't from another dimension, I think I could really like him. As it is, I don't know him that well at all. Although the girls in all those fantasy novels I've read didn't seem to have any problem with it, as long as the guy was hot. But then again, I could be reading him all wrong. Maybe he's just fascinated by the fact that I'm not from Meynch. Abi sighed. *Too much stress. I'll feel better in the morning.* Abi's eyes slowly closed as she relaxed her body, and soon she fell fast asleep, turning over on her side to hug her pillow.

Unknown to Abi, a phantom that glowed golden white light watched her tenderly. She was ignorant of the true reason behind the unrest in Meynch, and the only way the prophecy would be fulfilled was to give her a glimpse of the hidden realm. So it patiently waited, biding its time…

The Vision

Abi's eyes flew open. *Where am I?* she thought.

She looked around. She was in a dome-shaped building that reminded her of the Pantheon in Rome or the Jefferson Memorial in Washington, DC. Several huge columns at least fifty feet tall supported the ornately painted dome engraved with an image of two glowing beings in battle—one with a shining sword, the other with a darkened one. The image gave her the sensation that this chamber held an ancient power, and she knew that she had been brought here for a reason.

There were no walls, but all around her were bookshelves filled with books. There were books of every size and color, but one in particular drew her gaze. Unlike all the others, it seemed to glow with an aura of power and importance. Abi was drawn to the book as if it was calling her, beckoning her to reveal its secrets. She took the book off the shelf and opened it to the first page.

"Deep within the mountains of Troche, the castle of Aadonai was nestled," Abi read aloud. "There lived a King cloaked in mystery whom the people called the Shepherd. No one knew his real name or where he had come from. To them he had always been there. He always listened to the peoples' complaints—peasants and lawmen alike. He was fair and merciful in all his laws and made sure justice was shown. For many years, peace prevailed in the land.

"The King had married Lorna, a beautiful young lady who was abandoned at birth. But she was unfaithful to him and betrayed the King with her many lovers from faraway lands. As a righteous King, he could not continue their relationship in light of her infidelity, so the King sent her away with a heavy heart.

"Then one day a young man appeared on the king's doorstep and claimed he was the Shepherd's Son. He admitted that Lorna had given birth to him after the King sent her away, but he insisted that he was the Shepherd's offspring.

"'What proof do you have of this claim?' the King asked.

The young man stepped close to the throne, and when the guards made a move to stop him, the King waved them aside. The two shared a long, meaningful look, and everyone there knew something much more powerful than words passed between them.

"Whatever was revealed in that look convinced the King of the young man's honesty, for he quickly made him Prince of the realm. The young man soon proved himself pure of heart and mind.

"Soon afterward, the King summoned the Prince. He told his son that he had become too old to visit the people as he used to. So many people assumed the King was dead or did not care about them anymore. But for the few people who still loved the King, the only connection to him were his laws. The lawmen had become drunk with their power and influence over the people, and it had corrupted them. They had become ruthless in upholding the laws. The King asked the young Prince to dismiss the present lawmen from their positions and find righteous men to replace them.

"So the Prince traveled down the mountains to the town of Meynch and lived there for several years. He told everyone that he was the King's son who had come to release them from the burden of oppression the lawmen had placed upon their shoulders.

"'For my yoke is easy, and my burden is light,' the Prince said.

"Though he spoke of peace and honesty among men, he gained many enemies among the lawmen who loathed him so much that they would do anything to get rid of him. When the Prince died, everyone in Meynch suspected the lawmen, but they insisted that he died of a heart attack."

Abi turned the page for the rest of the story, but it ended there. On the next page, she saw a poem written in flowing, golden cursive, and she read it silently.

> Children come from other worlds,
>
> They come to show the truth at last.
>
> Secrets hidden, friends unknown,
>
> They reveal the evil veiled.
>
> Wanderer's children find a home,
>
> Yet do not know their past,
>
> They must cast aside all doubts,

And bow before the Shepherd King.

As she reached the end of the page, the poem shimmered then transformed into a picture of a great throne room. Abi gingerly touched it, and a sensation similar to heat lightning coursed through her. Her hand was sucked into the picture, and she couldn't seem to move as her body was sucked in as well—the picture becoming clearer and clearer until it seemed she was actually there.

All at once, the tingling sensation disappeared, and Abi looked at her hands, which were still cradling the book. But she wasn't in the library anymore. She was in the throne room she had seen in the book, and she was a silent spectator, watching the scene unfold before her.

A regal-looking elderly man on a radiant, golden throne spoke softly to a handsome younger man who was dressed in elegant robes.

"I will miss you, my son. Be careful." The man's gaze was tender but sad as he looked at the young man.

"Don't worry, Father. I go to assure them that you still care about them even though they haven't heard from you for many years. I know that there are some who do not want to hear my message, but there are many more who do. They need the hope I offer."

When it looked like his father was going to protest, the young Prince stepped forward to embrace the King and walked to the huge, golden door. As he opened the door, his father called, "Take care."

"Good-bye, Papa." The Prince looked as if he would say something else, but he just bit his lip and brushed something from his eyes. Then he disappeared through the doorway.

"I love you, my son," the King whispered.

The scene faded, and Abi was again in the library. Abi felt the King's grief at letting his son walk willingly into such a dangerous situation, and knowing the end of the story only increased her sadness and sympathy. She looked down at the book and saw that the poem had appeared again. She touched the glowing words in the book and gasped. There were four new lines! As tingles flew up and down her arm, she closed her eyes, ready to see another vision.

A Prince gave up his noble crown;

A Stranger's death brought life.

Child, prepare the people's hearts

For the Prince will come again.

What Next?

Abi's eyes fluttered open. She looked around. This was not her bedroom...why were there two beds, and who was the girl sleeping in the other bed?

Where am I?

An instant later, the events of the past two days came rushing back to her. She realized she was in her room at Kes's house. It had just been another vision.

She sighed—*with disappointment*, she realized. Though the visions were startling and came at the most unexpected times, she enjoyed the sense of purpose they gave her. *This is even better than the daydreams I used to have. These are actually real! I'm like, a pyschic or something! It's pretty awesome.*

Her eyelids started to droop, and she yawned. In the eerie quiet of her room, it sounded like an air raid siren. She giggled softly and then stiffened as Weana stirred fitfully. Abi sat up, swung her legs over the bed, and tiptoed to Weana's bed. Humming softly, Abi tried to calm her cousin and lull her back to sleep. Eventually, Weana's breathing was even and peaceful again.

Abi tiptoed back to her bed, so as not to wake Weana. She paused, though, and looked out the window at the rising sun. She sat down in a small chair beside the window and attempted to organize all her chaotic thoughts into sensible questions.

Will we ever find the Stranger? And even if we do, will he be able to get us home? And what about our family?

Now that we know we were born in Meynch, how will it affect us as a family? What about the lawmen here? They are hiding too many secrets for my liking, especially Micah. It's so sad how he broke off his friendship with Dad. Maybe there is still some good in him.

Abi was so deep in thought that she didn't hear the door open slightly behind her and a figure enter, tip-toeing to a spot beside her. She heard the door creak as it closed, though, and jerked around to see Chris, grinning broadly.

"Abi, did I ever tell you that you have horrible reflexes?"

"Hey, I was thinking. I wasn't paying attention," Abi said defensively.

"Well, not paying attention could cost you your life. What if it wasn't me behind you but a lawman ready to kill you?"

Abi just glared at him in response.

"You're grumpy this early?" Chris joked, but seeing Abi's narrowed eyes, backed off immediately. "Whoa, sorry." He pulled up another chair beside her and asked comfortingly, "What's wrong?"

Abi sighed. "I'm so confused. I thought all we had to do was ask around, and people would give so much information we'd know exactly where the Stranger was. Then he'd create another portal, send us back home, and everything would be back to normal…"

Chris finished her thought. "But you didn't count on the lawmen, and there was no way you could have known that we would find out that we were born in another dimension."

"Yeah. So what are we going to do now?"

"Well, Kes and Marla would probably let us stay with them until it's safe to go out in public again. We are fugitives, remember?"

"And another thing. Am I the only one who is thinking that their reaction to us being strangers is a little extreme? I can understand being suspicious, but arresting us just because they think we're not from here is a little much."

"It's because of the Stranger. Whatever he did really messed them up on every other Stranger, or at least that's what Kes said, remember?"

Chris sighed. "We seem to be traveling in a circle. We're exactly back where we started with no more knowledge about the Stranger than we had in the beginning."

Something about his last statement bothered Abi, and she struggled to place it. Then she remembered. "Chris, we *do* have more information! Remember I told you about the visions I have sometimes?" Chris opened his mouth to speak, but Abi didn't notice and continued talking. "Well, I had one last night, and..." She proceeded to tell him about her dream. He looked skeptical at first, but when she finally finished, it was almost time for breakfast, and he looked convinced.

"All right, so the Stranger is the Son of the Shepherd King. The Stranger died, the lawmen were happy, and his body was never found. That just confirms Micah's story," Chris said.

"Not really. Micah said that the Stranger *claimed* to be the King's Son. He didn't admit the Stranger really *was* the King's Son. And he never mentioned that people suspected the lawmen of killing him."

"My point is, we're right where we were before. The Stranger is still dead, we're still in Meynch, and the lawmen are still out to get us."

Abi sighed and got up from her chair by the window to collapse on her bed. "There's got to be *some* way to find the Stranger. We wouldn't have been sent here if it was impossible, yet we just keep finding more questions than answers."

"There's something we are missing—something important. I can feel it. There's one big piece of information that we don't have..."

A heavy silence descended as they both contemplated what was missing.

ARRESTED!

A loud bell interrupted their thoughts, and Marla's voice echoed through the house. "Children, time for breakfast! Hurry before it gets cold."

Abi sat up and jumped off the bed. Chris ran to the door to go to his room, but when he opened the door, the smell of waffles and pancakes drifted through the room. "Mmm! That smells delicious." He turned to Abi. "I'm going to go get dressed. See you downstairs," and Chris ran to his room.

Abi grinned at the door for a moment. *Chris and his appetite,* she thought. She shook her head and turned to her own closet. But before she could pick her outfit, she heard Weana stir. "Abi?" she murmured.

Abi went to Weana's bed. "Yes, Weana?"

"Is it breakfast time?"

"Yes, it is," Abi replied.

Weana burst out of bed in a flurry of purple and green polka-dotted sheets and blankets. "Let's go!" She ran to her closet and rummaged through it, throwing a scarlet dress with pink stars, yellow pants, and orange socks on the floor.

"Whoa, girl. Slow down!" Abi picked up the dress. "This dress will look pretty on you, but not with these pants and socks." Abi continued to give Weana some fashion advice, and soon Weana was dressed presentably.

Abi stepped back and admired her for a moment. *Weana will be a knockout in a couple years*, she thought.

Her cousin's wavy, strawberry-blond hair and delicate features were already attractive even at the tender age of nine.

Abi smiled at her. "Go downstairs now and eat breakfast. Tell your mom that I'm getting ready and will be right down."

Weana nodded and went out the door, closing it behind her. Abi turned to her closet. All of a sudden, she felt a nagging feeling as if something was wrong. She heard no voices downstairs, and the house was deathly quiet. A loud, high-pitched scream pierced the silence only to be muffled suddenly. *Weana!* Abi ran out, grabbing a robe that hung from the closet.

She looked over the railing to see what was wrong, and her eyes widened. She crouched quickly behind the bars of the railing and looked in horror at the scene before her. Marla, Kes, and her father stood gagged and bound. They were being led outside by three big, burly men. The men's backs were to Abi, but their black, leather jackets had a patch that said in bold black letters, *Lawmen Police*. Weana, tears running down her face, was attempting to run to her parents, but another man restrained her with one hand over her mouth, muffling her sobs.

"Where are the Stranger brats?" The man holding Abi's uncle raised a fist and drilled his malevolent gaze into Kes.

"I told you, they stopped here and kept running toward the mountains. They said something about finding the King." Kes didn't blink once as he repeated a calm, matter-of-fact lie.

The man's eyes narrowed. "You," he pointed to one of the other men who stood behind him, "look upstairs."

"No!" Kes shouted, and the men glared at him. "I have valuables up there, and I don't want you going through them. You have no right to invade my privacy, especially when I've told you all I know."

For a moment, Abi was afraid the men would come upstairs anyway, but the man motioned for his partner to stop. "You're not a troublemaker, usually. So I'll go by your words if you and your family come with us peacefully. But if I find out you've been lying to me, I will be back to burn your house to the ground."

Abi covered her mouth and turned away, crying softly. She gently opened Chris's door. She had to warn him!

Chris was tugging on his shoes when Abi opened his door. He looked up and was about to question her, but her shaking shoulders and tear-tracked cheeks silenced him.

"Chris! Marla, Kes, and Dad are…are…" She faltered.

Chris came to stand beside her and looked over her shoulder through the doorway. He couldn't see much, but what he could see made his teeth clench. He went back into his room and pulled Abi further in, cautiously closing the door behind them.

He looked at her, his anger at the lawmen spilling into his eyes. "We've got to do something!"

"Don't you see? We're the reason they came! The only reason Marla, Kes, and Weana are in this mess is because they helped us and gave us a place to stay!"

"What about Dad? Abi, we have to help them. We have to do something!" Chris repeated in frustration.

Abi sniffed and wiped her eyes with the back of her hand. "I know. I want to help them, too, but we can't just go charging downstairs and get ourselves arrested, too. We need a plan."

Just then a door opened, and Abi and Chris swerved to look at the bedroom door, but it hadn't moved. Chris turned back and saw Nathan emerging out of the bedroom's bathroom with a grin on his face. He glanced at Chris's anger-filled face and Abi's tear-streaked one, and his grin faded. "What happened?" he asked.

"The lawmen arrested Marla, Kes, our dad, and Weana and took them away," Chris said, his voice cracking as he struggled back the sudden tears.

Nathan closed his eyes for a moment. When he opened them, his eyes looked like blue granite. Abi saw the fun-loving boy disappear to be replaced with someone she didn't recognize. His jaw was clenched, and he spoke in a tight voice. "We have to get them back."

Abi shuddered. She was more worried about Nathan's steely rage than her brother's impulsiveness. She walked up to him and put a tender hand on his shoulder. "Nathan, calm down. We need a plan." She looked up at him pleadingly, her eyes shining with unshed tears that were threatening to spill over.

Nathan looked down at her impassively then, slowly, his jaw loosened, and his eyes became a little softer. He sighed, then pulled her into a quick embrace. Abi relaxed against him for a brief, forbidden moment, and then he gently pushed her away.

He looked down into her eyes, answering her unspoken question. He would take control. He knew this town forward and backward, and could easily figure out a way to get to where the lawmen took their friends and family while staying out of sight. "You're right. We need a plan."

The "Explosion" and Its Effects

Nathan put his finger over his lips, motioned for Abi and Chris to crouch down, and carefully, quietly opened the door. There was no sound from downstairs, but that did not guarantee that the lawmen were gone. He turned back to Abi and Chris.

"Someone's going to have to go to the railing and see what's going on," he said softly.

Chris nodded and pointed to himself, but Abi shook her head violently, mouthing, "Let me go." Nathan pressed his lips together, and his eyes darted from Abi to the door and back to Abi. Chris frowned at her, but Abi's face had become expressionless. Nathan sighed and slowly nodded. Chris looked at him with wide eyes and was certain Nathan had just pronounced Abi's death sentence. Abi whispered, "I'll be back. Don't worry."

Abi lay on her stomach, slid through the barely open door, and, inch by inch, crawled to the railing. When she was only a few feet away, she looked through the posts. There was no one. Or was there? A quick movement caught her eye. A friendly signal? Maybe. An intruder's threat? She didn't know. It disappeared when Abi tried to focus on it, and it had come and gone so quickly she couldn't identify what it was or where it was coming from.

Abi crawled back to the room to report quietly, "There was no one in the rooms, but I think I saw someone hiding."

Chris softly closed the door then turned to her. "Are you sure? Those men didn't look like they'd let anyone escape." He got to his feet, and so did Abi and Nathan, stretching their legs gingerly.

"It might have been one of the lawmen. They might have been assigned to guard the house or something," Abi said as she looked to Nathan for confirmation.

But Nathan only nodded absently and tapped his index finger against his chin, deep in thought. After a long moment of silence, Nathan finally spoke. "Honestly? Usually this is when the buff hero cracks a joke about the situation and makes the pretty girl laugh, and then both guys fearlessly defeat all the bad guys and rescue the captives. But I'm having a hard time coming up with a silver lining…and I haven't really exercised in a while."

Abi almost laughed, more out of nervousness than anything else, but Chris did not even crack a smile. His expression was furious. "You think?" he said to Nathan. "The lawmen are out to get us, we are *completely* alone because everyone we trusted has been arrested, and we have no clue what to do to find them. Oh, and, by the way, Abi and I can't ever leave this place until we find a man who's been dead for years!" Chris raked his hand angrily through his sandy, brown hair, his hazel eyes flashing. "There's no silver lining, period."

Abi was really starting to worry. Her brother so far had been pretty calm about this whole situation, and his acceptance had kept her from completely freaking out. She did not know what she would do if he broke under all the stress. "Come on, big brother! Pull it together! We'll find—"*Boom!*

A loud peal resonated through the house, interrupting Abi's encouragement. The immense sound waves knocked Abi off her feet, but Chris and Nathan immediately dropped to lie on their stomachs before they were affected. The door closed with a bang as a powerful wind swept through the room.

"It's an earthquake!" Chris yelled. The sound faded away almost instantly after Chris's exclamation, and they all stood up again, being a little unsteady.

"Is anybody hurt?" Nathan asked.

Chris shook his head, and Abi was about to do the same, but a sudden ache in her back stopped her. She touched it lightly with her palm and winced at the pain. "I think I hurt my back," she said. She felt around on the floor and found a sharp shard of Weana's broken glass jewelry box on the floor. "On this," she added.

"Is it bleeding?"

Abi looked at her palm. It had blood smeared on it—not a lot, but enough for her to be concerned. "A little."

"We have bandages downstairs." Nathan turned to Chris. "Chris, when you go into the kitchen, next to the oven there are three drawers. The one on the top has bandages. Bring the whole box."

"What about the person Abi said was hiding downstairs?"

"We are just going to have to risk it. Abi, lean forward so I can see the wound," Nathan instructed, looking slightly uncomfortable. "I'll have to pull up your shirt a bit."

"It's okay," Abi said, her cheeks flushing in embarrassment. *This is awkward.* Abi leaned forward, and Nathan, with an apologetic look at Abi, pulled up the back of her shirt slightly and stared at her back. "It's bleeding a lot, but I don't think it's as awful as it could be. Glass often causes really deep wounds, but fortunately you fell on top of the flat part of the shard, not the edge."

"Abi, are you going to be okay?" Chris asked, a tinge of concern in his voice.

"I'll be fine. Ow!" Abi winced at the sudden sting as Nathan wiped her back with a wet paper towel he had just retrieved from his bathroom.

Chris nodded and gingerly opened the door to go downstairs but paused midway, his jaw going slack. At the doorway stood Weana with her dress torn and hair in disarray, her hand covering something on her cheek.

"What happened?" Nathan asked compassionately.

Weana limped inside. "When I went downstairs, the lawmen had captured Mom and Dad and Uncle Scott. One man grabbed me, too, but when the lawmen took us, Daddy distracted the lawmen so I could get away and hide. The lawmen couldn't find me, so they left. Later, I saw Abi hiding upstairs, and I tried to get her to see me. But I wasn't sure she did." Weana turned to Abi with a questioning expression.

"I saw something, but I wasn't sure it was you," Abi said.

"Then the explosion came from behind me and pushed me into the couch." Weana pulled up her pants to reveal a thin gash on her leg from her knee to her ankle. It had already stopped bleeding. "My leg got caught underneath the couch leg, but a sharp part on the bottom cut my cheek. It hurts more than my leg." She moved her hand away from her cheek for a moment to reveal a small but wide gash on her right cheek that bled freely.

Abi gasped and Chris's eyes widened, but Nathan just nodded. "That's probably because it's deeper than the cut on your leg. Chris, get lots of bandages. I'm not sure how many Abi's back and Weana's cheek will need."

After Chris left, Abi drew Weana into a comforting hug. "You were very brave to run away from the lawmen and hide," Abi whispered in Weana's ear.

Weana dipped her head. "I didn't cry when I cut my leg, but I cried a little when I cut my cheek. Is that okay?"

"That is absolutely fine. Everyone cries when they are hurt. Ow!" Abi yelled. Nathan winced and said apologetically, "Sorry." He finished wiping Abi's back just as Chris arrived with two rolls of bandages.

"Here are some bandages," Chris said.

"Great! Pass me some," Nathan requested. He gave them to Abi and told her to go to the bathroom and attempt to wrap the dressing around her torso. "The wound is midway down your back, near your…

umm…bra," he stammered. "I would help you, but…" He blushed and grinned sheepishly. "While you're doing that, I'll help Weana." Abi nodded and went in the bathroom.

"How do *you* know so much about doctoring?" Chris asked Nathan.

Nathan shrugged and said casually, "I used to want to be a doctor. But my dad, before he died, said he wanted me to be a merchant, and to ignore the last wishes of a dying man is considered a crime. So I was apprenticed to Kes."

"Oh, I'm sorry."

"Don't be. Kes is a wonderful master. He has taught me a lot." And with that, Nathan effectively closed the subject to further discussion.

Tension

Ten minutes later, the door opened and Abi came out.

"Everything okay?" Chris asked.

Nathan checked her bandage. "Yes, she bound it well. It looks like the bleeding has decreased. Abi, you should be fine. Just try not to do any stretching for a while."

"Okay. How's Weana?" Abi turned to see Nathan placing a stick-on, square cloth bandage on Weana's right cheek. "Is she going to be all right?"

"Yes, she'll be fine, too. It's a little deep, but it won't need stitches," Nathan answered. Suddenly he gasped and hit his head with his palm. "Oh, I almost forgot! I'm such a idiot!" He turned to Chris. "Chris, did you see anyone downstairs? Maybe a lawman or a spy from the lawmen?"

"I didn't," Chris replied, "but I was only there for a couple minutes. Weana would probably know."

"Oh. Right. Sorry. Weana, did you see anyone downstairs?"

Weana shook her head. "No, I didn't. But when the lawmen were looking for me, I heard them talking. Some of the stuff they said might be useful." Her eyes fluttered, and she paled.

Abi sensed that her young cousin was barely holding herself together. If Abi was in Weana's shoes right now and had seen her parents hauled away, she would have broken down and had herself a good cry right about now. Yet Weana had maintained her composure amazingly well for being so young.

Nathan, seeming to realize the same thing, sat down and patted the space on the floor next to him. “Come sit down, Weana. We’ll figure everything out.”

Weana looked at them gratefully. “Thanks. This is all so scary, but I know you guys will help me. Daddy said I could trust you.”

Nathan sat down opposite of Abi, and Chris sat down next to Abi, putting a comforting arm around Weana. Abi smiled at her brother. *I admit it. He* can *be really sweet when he wants to be.*

“Well, they were talking about the Stranger’s friends and how they said something about the Stranger coming back soon…” Weana began, but Abi didn’t hear the rest. The scene in front of her seemed to fade, and Abi rubbed her eyes and looked again. *I’m having another vision,* Abi thought excitedly. She closed her eyes so she could see more clearly…

The Plot Thickens

Twelve men sat around a large round table, reminding Abi of King Arthur and his knights. One broad-shouldered man with long, wavy, fiery red hair stood up and addressed the group.

"Friends, I have called you together for a reason—to prepare for the return of the Prince." He seemed about to continue, but another man stood up. Abi stared intently at him. He seemed familiar.

"Jonathan, we know the Prince said he would come back soon. And we all eagerly await his return," the man said dryly. "But the Prince said that the Three Prophecies must be fulfilled before he comes."

"Micah, Micah, if you had but waited, I would have told you why I say we must prepare. The First of the Three Prophecies has been fulfilled!"

Abi gasped. *Micah was the lawman who tricked us! He's a friend of the Stranger!*

Another man stood up. "Impossible!" Beefy and red-faced, the pudgy man looked like a ticking time bomb of emotions. "The First Prophecy is…"

A booming voice interrupted them all. "Peace!"

All three men sat down immediately, and everyone stared at the broad, wooden doorway through which a burly figure dressed in a dark, hooded cloak entered. Once he entered the light, he removed his hood. Black hair framed skin the color of deep, rich chocolate and piercing dark eyes. This man was obviously older than the rest of the men, and the wisdom of many years shone in his kind face. But he didn't look like someone who had the resounding voice that had calmed the three men so quickly.

Jonathan stood slowly and bowed. "With respect, I bow, Seginus. What brings you to our table?"

The man, Seginus, looked at each one at the table in turn, but suddenly he seemed to look right at Abi. She stiffened. *Did he see me? I didn't think anyone in my vision could see me.* But he soon turned back to Jonathan, and Abi breathed a sigh of relief.

"I came because I have also heard that the First Prophecy has been fulfilled. I have seen them myself. They have come."

A young man, who was barely older than Chris, stood up. "Pardon me, but I have just joined the Prince's followers, and I am not familiar with these Three Prophecies. Pray tell what they are."

Seginus nodded and began,

"The first is,

Children come from other worlds,

They come to show the truth at last.

Secrets hidden, friends unknown,

They reveal the evil veiled.

Wanderer's children find a home,

Yet do not know their past,

They must cast aside all doubts,

And bow before the Shepherd King.

"The second,

A father's delight, his life

Ripped from his tender arms.

Living two separate lives

With aching in their hearts.

Stranger children come once more

To reunite a clan.

But what they find will change the fate

Of more than just one land.

"And the final of the Three Prophecies,

Evil powers called upon

Cause havoc through the land.

One man tries to overthrow

The King's mighty hand.

Dimensions shift, worlds collide,

Earth is earth no more.

Stranger children, your last chance,

Or both our worlds will perish.

As Seginus ended the poems, Abi realized something. *The first prophecy was in my vision last night!* She listened carefully now.

The red-faced man stood up again, bowing to Seginus, then asking in a calmer voice than before, "So you are suggesting that the children of prophecy, the stranger children, are in Meynch now?"

"I am not suggesting it. I am saying it. They have already met Micah," Seginus glanced at Micah, but Micah did not acknowledge this, "and are now in hiding until it is their time. Did any of you feel the explosion? That was no ordinary explosion. It was a sign. But in the present company," Seginus again looked at Micah, "I will not say more for fear the information would fall into the wrong hands."

Jonathan obviously saw the tension between Seginus and Micah. *A blind man could see that Seginus doesn't trust Micah,* Abi thought. *And for good reason, though he probably doesn't know it.* "Micah, you may go now," Jonathan said after an awkward moment. "We will dismiss in a moment, and we don't want to keep you away from your duties." Micah reluctantly left the assembly but not without a surly nod to Seginus. Micah's failure to bow was noticed by everyone, including Seginus and Jonathan.

Jonathan dismissed the group, but he and Seginus stayed behind. "I don't like it," Seginus said quietly to Jonathan. He had walked to stand beside Jonathan at a window where they could see Micah's retreating form."I wish we could find out for sure if Micah's a lawman, but if we do, we risk exposing ourselves. But even if he isn't a lawman, he has the conceited air of one. I don't trust him as far I could throw him."

Jonathan chuckled. "With all due respect, that wouldn't be far. Your old bones can barely move an inch."

Seginus grinned at Jonathan. "Exactly!" But he sobered as he looked back outside. "Still, don't say anything about who the children are and where they are now. I'm pretty sure he has suspicions, but he doesn't know for sure, and I intend to keep it that way."

The scene changed, and Abi recognized Micah's cottage. A devious-looking, hunchbacked man walked quickly toward it, his eyes darting from side to side. As he drew nearer to the cottage and to Abi, who was standing in front of it, she could tell he was not Micah. His shoulders were too thin and his face too angular. But his eyes… Abi shuddered. His eyes were pure black with flecks of blue steel—narrowed and suspicious, hard and cruel.

Yet what gave Abi chills was the something lurking behind his eyes. It was powerful, and it was evil—hideously evil. But it disappeared quickly, leaving Abi wondering if it was just her imagination.

Too many things are uncertain in Meynch, she thought. *The people here trust no one and live in too much fear. But I think they fear more than just the lawmen, but who—or what—is it? And does it have anything to do with what I have just seen?*

As she was deep in thought, she abruptly felt herself move not of her own will toward the cottage door. She attempted to stop, but she had about the same effect on her surroundings as a ghost. If she could not move, and this force kept pushing her, she would slam into the cottage wall. She shut her eyes and waited for the impact.

Abi felt herself stop. Did I stop in front of the cottage? She opened one eye cautiously. She recognized the room where they had met Micah the other day. *What happened?* She turned, being aided by an invisible hand. The door was behind her. *That means I must have gone through the door!* She blinked in surprise but then shrugged. *Well, I might as well be a ghost because solid humans can't go through doors and aren't invisible.*

She turned back to the room and focused on it. Gradually, people appeared in the room like a fuzzy lens slowly becoming clear. One of them was Micah, and the other was the man she had seen outside the cottage. They were whispering, and at first Abi had to strain to hear, but suddenly every word became crystal clear.

"So those children who escaped from your prisons, the ones whom you underestimated in your pride and stupidity, calling them nothing but young troublemakers, those children are the children of the prophecies?" The man pronounced every word calmly, but explosive anger simmered beneath the surface.

Micah winced and bent his head. "I'm sorry, Judge Faln." But the gleam in his eyes was far from submissive. Abi saw it, and evidently Judge Faln saw it, too, but he made no comment until Micah added, "I was doing exactly as you told me to."

That did it. Judge Faln straightened to his full height, and his eyes lit with blazing violet flames. "How dare you imply that I made a error in judgment!" He leaned nearer to Micah, and his voice deepened as he whispered in Micah's ear, "I have power beyond what you can comprehend and influence beyond anything you can ever imagine."

Abi shivered. These visions were trying to show her something, but what? Suddenly the scene became hazy and faded away, and Abi was in a room she recognized as the library from her previous dreams. She looked around, not sure of what to do next.

A glowing parchment caught her eye as she scanned the room. She walked quickly toward it. As she drew nearer, she realized it was a worn, ancient-looking scroll with elegant script. She read it silently to herself.

"For we do not wrestle against flesh and blood, but against the rulers, against the authorities, against the cosmic powers over this present darkness, against the spiritual forces of evil in the heavenly places."

She sat down on the carpeted floor. Is there someone—or some ones—else controlling Meynch?

Are they some sort of spiritual beings? Are they evil?

Did the Stranger's arrival disturb their hold on the people? Is that why the lawmen were so desperate to kill him?

Are there also good beings that are on the Stranger's side? Was the unrest in Meynch not because of the Stranger but because the evil powers controlling the lawmen feared the good powers that arrived with the Stranger? Were the peasants and merchants just bystanders who had to choose sides?

Abi rubbed her temples. The plot was getting thicker, and she couldn't keep up. *I'll just close my eyes for a moment. I always think better with my eyes closed…*

Connecting the Dots

"Abi? Abi, can you hear me?" Chris's voice trembled. He was on the verge of tears. He knelt beside Abi, calling her name and shaking her. She was pale and still, but there was still a pulse. Nathan and Weana sat around them, worry etched on their faces, as well.

Weana had been telling them about what she had seen and heard while she was hiding from the lawmen, when Abi suddenly became limp and fell backward. Chris caught her before she could hit her head against the hard floor, and he picked up her lifeless form and gently stretched her out on his bed. Weana stopped mid-sentence and scurried to Abi's side, and Nathan's face, which was seemingly etched out of stone before, had softened to a look of concern as he came to help.

"She's alive," Nathan pronounced after looking her over, "but she seems to be unconscious."

"I could have told you that," Chris commented. Nathan's solemn face had silenced him, and Chris now stared with apprehension at Abi's ashen countenance. Would she ever wake up? Was she having another vision? He kept his questions to himself. He paced the floor as Nathan and Weana knelt by Abi's bedside.

A moan arose from the bed, disturbing Chris's thoughts. Abi moaned again, and Chris quickly came to her side. "Abi! Abi, can you hear me?" he said urgently.

Abi's eyes slowly opened. "Chris?" she said drowsily.

"Yeah, it's me. Are you okay?" Chris asked.

"What happened?"

"You collapsed while Weana was talking."

"What?" Abi gingerly rubbed her temples, struggling to remember the past few minutes. Then everything she had seen came rushing back to her. Abi's eyes widened, and she suddenly sat up on the bed. "I remember! Chris, I had another vision, and this one is important."

"You can talk about it later," Nathan interrupted. "Abi, you need to recover your strength. You fainted, and you can't just pop out of bed like nothing happened."

Abi ignored him. "Guys, I have been having visions ever since right before I came to Meynch. They all were scenes in somebody else's life. I've seen the lawmen, the Stranger's friends, the Shepherd King, and the Stranger, who is the Prince. In this vision, I saw the Stranger's friends, and they were talking about some prophecies that told that Chris and I were coming. Then I saw Micah with the Stranger's friends. He's a spy for the lawmen. He went to Judge Faln, who is a really spooky guy, by the way, and told him everything the Stranger's friends said.

"But the scroll said something about not fighting against people but against the cosmic powers of darkness or something like that. I think evil beings are controlling the lawmen who control Meynch. When the Stranger came, he brought good powers, and as he reached out to the people, the evil powers' hold on the people through the lawmen was shaken. That's why the lawmen were so desperate to kill him, because the evil beings didn't want to be overthrown by the good beings." Abi paused, suddenly becoming aware that everyone was staring at her. "Did I go too fast?" she asked.

And just when I was starting to think we solved all the mysteries in Meynch. Chris sighed. "I think I get the gist. Basically, we're dealing with *Harry Potter* come to life. All that's missing is Voldemort, Dumbledore, and some Death Eaters. Wait, so does that mean we can use magic wands now?"

Abi rolled her eyes. "Really? You really had to say that? Do you always have to crack a joke?"

Nathan raised an eyebrow, looking more than a little puzzled. "Uh, I have no idea what you guys are talking about. But ever since the Stranger came, there have been weird things happening. Something bad has happened to everyone who supported him, and I overheard Kes and Marla wondering if we would be next. But then you came. You don't know the effect you had and still are having on this town. I only heard a fraction of it at the market, but everyone is talking about you.

"The prophecy you mentioned? It's one of the only things that the lawmen can't adjust to fit their own purposes. It's been around for centuries. No one knows who said it, but a couple years ago the Stranger repeated it, saying, 'The young men of this generation will not die before this prophecy is fulfilled,' or something like that. Then *bam!* You guys came. The something that's controlling them must hate the Stranger and you, and it probably wants to get rid of both threats."

"And we are going to," a voice behind them said.

Abi's eyes widened. Chris's jaw dropped. Nathan couldn't breathe.

UNITED WE STAND

A man stood in the doorway, blocking their escape, while Judge Faln looked over his captives. "So you are the famous children of prophecy. I admit, I expected you to be a little...well, smarter." He smirked at Abi and Chris. "I expected this to be a match of equal forces. I thought you would be both amazingly intelligent for your age and charismatic leaders who would immediately step up and challenge me. But, sadly, you have disappointed me."

Nathan spat at the judge's feet and earned himself a stinging slap. "Don't sass your elders, boy," Judge Faln said coolly. He turned back to Abi and Chris.

"So you figured out the *real* power here in Meynch. Good for you. I expect for you to know exactly what you're up against." His voice deepened, and it seemed another being was speaking. "Let me simplify it for you, children." He said the word *children* like it was a dirty word. "We have reigned for centuries unchallenged, and we don't intend to let riffraff change that. You probably know about the Shepherd..." the voice hesitated, and Judge Faln coughed, "...the Stranger's Father. His power over the people was hard to overthrow, but eventually He lost touch, and we took over.

"Scott, your bothersome father, worried us for a while, but he *ended serving* our purposes by bringing our greatest ally, Reilim. The Stranger, though, was too troublesome to ignore. He has stirred up the people, and they are even now questioning us and our authority. His death did nothing, unfortunately, to control the suspicion and rumors about our supposed 'oppression.' And now you…children have arrived." Judge Faln sneered at them. "We will not allow you to find the Stranger. It will not happen."

Abi and Chris stared up at him and were angry but powerless. The moment he had begun addressing them, before Abi and Chris even had time to react, his men had seized them and tied them up, throwing them on the floor when they were finished. They were bound back-to-back and wrist-to-wrist on the floor, and they had to twist their heads to see Judge Faln. His dark-blue eyes looked black as a malevolent presence stared back at them for a moment. They shivered.

"Yes, be afraid. You will not escape me this time. You may have power, but I have spirits at my command. You will die here in Meynch along with your equally annoying family." He glanced at Nathan. "But you. You have nothing to do with them. You were just in the wrong place at the wrong time, yes? Renounce your ties to these ruffians, and I'm sure I can clear your record and forgive you this one offense." Faln stared deeply into Nathan's eyes. "What do you say, boy? Their life or yours?"

Nathan cast a fleeting look at Abi and Chris. He was not bound like them—only held in the iron grip of a burly guard. It was obvious now why Faln had chosen to give him relatively better treatment.

Abi held Nathan's gaze, her eyes wide, though she did not speak. *Don't do it, Nathan. He's trying to divide us.*

Nathan struggled for a long, agonizing moment. *I might be able to get more help if I pretend to go along with the lawmen. But Abi and Chris and probably Kes, Marla, Weana, and Scott will hate me for being disloyal and abandoning them at their time of need. I don't want Abi to hate me! I have to stay with them!*

Are you doing this for her? Another voice intruded into his thoughts—a voice he did not recognize but instinctively trusted. *She is a wonderful girl, but she is not perfect. In times of danger, she is not the ultimate source of strength.*

Nathan's jaw firmed. No.

I'm doing this because I believe in the King.

I believe in the Stranger.

I believe that Abi and Chris were sent here for a purpose.

He spoke in a clear, determined voice. "I stand by Abi and Chris. I stand by the Stranger. I will not renounce the truth." He stared at Faln. "And I pity those who are willing to give up everything for lies."

Judge Faln glared at him, his eyes flaring. He made a motion to the guard, and he bound Nathan and threw him on the floor next to Abi and Chris. Nathan tried to squirm out of the rope, but it was tied tightly.

"I suppose you're waiting for me to say, 'Astonishing. Your courage is admirable. I am so inspired that I will set you free.'" Faln spoke in a falsetto voice, and his face was filled with mockery.

"That would be nice," Chris said with a half-grin.

Abi elbowed him. "Shut up!"

Judge Faln rolled his eyes. "So immature. If I were the King, I would be ashamed at such incompetent children of prophecy. It seems a waste to give obviously stupid children such an important mission." He turned to the burly guard that held Weana. She was treated even better than Nathan had been; the guard only held her arms lightly. "Take her away, but don't harm or abuse her." Seeing the guard's puzzled look, Faln said quickly, "We need her unharmed…"

The guard nodded, comprehending, and led Weana out.

"…otherwise I would indulge you," Judge Faln said to himself.

Abi shuddered. Treat someone by letting them inflict violence on innocent people? This man was inhuman! But her mind latched onto the "unharmed" part. She doubted her cousin's present safety was because of the kindness in Faln's heart, so what wicked plan would need Weana unharmed? And why her specifically? Abi's mind swirled with ideas.

The Interrogation

Judge Faln looked at Weana from over a small pile of books. He sat behind a wooden desk stacked high with papers. He knew he had to go about what he was about to do very delicately. Children were complex and unusually perceptive, so one wrong move could ruin everything.

"Weana, do you trust the boy and girl who came to Meynch about two days ago?"

"Yes." Her curt answer surprised Faln, but he didn't miss a beat.

"Do you know that they came from another world?"

"Yes." Weana played with the hem of her dress.

"Do you know that they were bad people in their world?"

If she was surprised at this, she didn't show it. *Remarkable to have mastered an impassive expression in only nine years,* he thought.

"It's not good to help bad people." Seeing the lie was not taking root, Judge Faln continued. "I'm afraid I have to punish you."

A flicker of fear shone in Weana's eyes for a moment but was quickly put out. But Faln saw it and was encouraged.

"Your parents also have to be punished." Faln made a motion to a guard behind Weana, and he disappeared. Seconds later, Kes was dragged in. He looked for the most part unhurt…except for several bruises on his face.

The fear in Weana's eyes was stronger now, and Faln decided it was time to take the next step. Most of his younger victims had broken at this point, crying for their parents, and had become so insufferable that he was forced to stop the investigation.

But this girl had grit. There was a good possibility that she would give him the information he needed. If she failed, it didn't matter. She was only a means to an end, but he could probably get the information elsewhere.

"Bring in the Enforcer."

A huge wooden contraption was pushed in the room by several well-built men. It resembled a giant scale that was complete with a platform on each side but seemed to operate manually by a wheel that was attached to the back of the column between the two platforms. One platform of the Enforcer had a plush couch surrounded by two wooden tables. The other platform had a cot that had chains attached to it. High above the cot was a knife hanging on a thick rope poised above the center of the cot.

Judge Faln escorted Weana to the platform with the couch. "Sit down here, my dear." He motioned to the guard who was holding Kes, and Kes was pushed onto the cot. Kes was compliant, and the guard's grip relaxed. But that was the opening Kes had been looking for. He broke away from the guard and ran for Weana.

Judge Faln's eyes flared, and he pointed at the door and quickly muttered a few words under his breath.

Dark shadows seemed to collect in the doorway, and an ominous rumble froze the already wide-eyed guards chasing Kes. But Kes kept running.

A sinister, arm-like shadow stretched out from the mass of darkness and barred the way to Weana, violet light flickering like electricity inside it. Kes looked at Judge Faln with a volatile mixture of anger and grief, bordering on insanity. Even Faln, as evil as he was, was momentarily taken aback by the depth of Kes's emotion. Kes continued toward Weana.

"No, Daddy, no!" But it was too late. Kes reached the smoky barrier and attempted to run through it. Kes's body jerked and twitched, and he fell limp to the floor only a few feet away from Weana. She tried to run to him, but the looming shadow blocked her. So all Weana could do was sit back down, and the velvet couch was stained by her silent tears.

Judge Faln nodded to the astonished guards, and they hesitantly picked up Kes's limp form and chained it to the cot. The shadows seemed to grow darker, still separating the area between Weana and Kes. Weana remained motionless, still sobbing quietly as she looked at her father's body.

"I'm sorry you had to see that," Faln whispered in her ear. He had moved to stand behind her, and he saw her shiver slightly from his warm breath. For a moment, he seriously considered his plans. She was such a pretty girl, except for that ugly cut on her cheek; maybe he could have some fun with her…

No! The sudden thought startled him and brought him back to his senses. This was no time for pleasure; he had a war to win, and the girl was just a pawn.

He stepped back and hid a smile. Everything was going according to plan.

"Now, this is what's going to happen. One of my men is going to turn this wheel slowly and bring this knife lower and closer to your father's heart."

Weana gasped softly.

"But that doesn't have to happen. You see, I need information about your cousins, where they go, and what they do. I need someone to be my informant. I could use one of my many lawmen, but to get the information I need, it would have to be someone your cousins trust. You would be the perfect person. To do this, I'd have to set you free, of course, but I would keep your parents and your Uncle Scott—as a guarantee, you understand."

"You evil, hateful, horrible old man!" Weana shrieked. "I would *never* betray my family!"

Faln shrugged. "If you change your mind, just tell me, and I will stop the imminent death your father will suffer."

He clapped his hands, and another burly guard began to turn the wheel. The rope lowered the knife inch by torturous inch. Weana stared at her father, willing him to move, to break away and run. But he didn't. He just lay there with his eyes closed—pale and deathly still.

When the knife was only a foot away from Kes, Weana broke down. She sobbed, her heart breaking, at the choice she had to make.

There was no one to help her. No one to deliver her. It was her heartache to bear no matter what she chose.

"Stop!" she shouted through her tears. "I've made my choice. But I won't say a word until you stop lowering the knife."

Faln immediately clapped his hand, and the wheel stopped. The rope was stretched taut above Kes's chest, and the knife was poised to plunge.

Oh Shepherd King, give me strength! But Weana knew that not even the King could help her now. Her sad yet determined eyes looked lovingly at her father's form.

Free at Last?

Abi, Chris, and Nathan sat in a prison cell, and each were deep in thought. Nathan was watching the guards pace in front of them. Suddenly he spoke, breaking the silence. "Twenty."

"What?"

"Twenty guards," Nathan said. "And they don't look nice. Or lax."

"So, Chris, do you have another *brilliant* escape plan yet?" Abi asked, sarcasm dripping from the word *brilliant*.

Nathan looked at Chris questioningly, but Chris shook his head. "You don't want to know," he whispered. He paused, then suddenly grinned, remembering. "You *really* don't want to know..."

Though she did not intend to, Abi giggled softly.

Suddenly the huge prison door that led outside flew open, and Judge Faln walked in, holding Weana's hand.

"Weana!" Nathan's quiet exclamation did not raise Weana's head. She apparently thought the designs on the floor tiles were more interesting than the safety of her friends. Or was it more than that?

"Weana?" Abi asked gently, somehow knowing there was more to her reluctance to look them in the eye than simply fear.

Weana looked up for a moment, and Abi was astonished and deeply disturbed by the deep-rooted anger and sadness that her eyes held.

"Good evening, children. Did you know today is my birthday?" Judge Faln's mocking voice interrupted Abi's dark thoughts.

No one responded.

"No? Well, I'm going to give you a present to celebrate." Faln held up the keys to their cell that had hung so close to their door, but even Chris hadn't been able to reach them through the bars. He slowly put a key in the lock and opened the cell door. "You're free!"

No one moved.

"You don't trust me?" Judge Faln put a hand over his heart and tried to look hurt. Somehow he only managed to look more sinister.

"No," Abi and Chris replied in unison.

"Good, because I don't trust you, either." Faln smirked evilly. "The only reason I'm setting you free is because you're more beneficial to me out there than in here. But your father, aunt, and uncle will stay with me for a little while longer. The rest of you are free to go!"

Two guards jogged into the cell and grabbed Abi and Chris's arms. "Oh, did I forget to mention Nathan? He stays with me, too." Faln frowned in mock sadness at Nathan. "So sorry, my boy."

Weana stared at the cell as the guards forced Abi and Chris out. They stood beside Weana and warily watched Judge Faln, thinking that this all seemed a little too tidy.

Why would Faln just let them go? Did it have anything to do with the anger Abi had seen in Weana's eyes? But with a not-so-subtle wink at Weana, Judge Faln left the prison. The guards followed—though not without locking the iron door between Nathan and his friends.

As the guards opened the door to leave, Chris suddenly jumped onto one of the guards and attempted to tackle him to the ground. The guard easily pushed him away but not before Chris grabbed something from the guard's belt. He quickly ran to stand beside Weana and held up his clenched fist at the guard. But the guard just sneered and turned away.

As soon as the prison door slammed shut, Chris opened his fist and grinned at Nathan. "I got it!"

Judge Faln waved all the guards away and quietly listened to the conversation through the door as the stranger children discussed their next step. He nodded occasionally then finally moved away. "Just as I thought," he muttered to himself. "No matter how gullible they obviously are, and in spite of their blunders, their mission is being guided by a higher power. That is the secret behind their success. Thankfully, they have become distracted and are blinded to the path before them, which buys us just enough time. Still, there are mighty powers at work here. Drastic measures need to be taken to ensure the desired result." He sighed deeply and closed his eyes, chanting words in a deep, powerful voice,

"Kaa, Spirit of Betrayal,

Hear my command,

The Light is what they seek,

But in the shadows they stand.

Darken their souls

And thwart their plan."

Faln paused and waited. Moments later, a sinister, deep voice rumbled that almost caused a small earthquake in the room. "Mortal, why have you disturbed me?"

"I am in need of your services. The children of prophecy have been loosed in the land, and they will disturb your reign if unhindered."

The voice rumbled again, and this time it almost sounded like a laugh. "Ahh…I now understand your presumptous summons. I find it amusing; therefore, I will not kill you yet. Who are you, a mere mortal, to command me, Kaa, the fallen spirit-ruler of the mountains?"

"Your Enemy seeks to use the children as weapons to end your reign in this world. His power is great. Is yours greater?"

This rumble sounded like a growl. "You push my generosity. Do not test me, mortal. It is according to my will whether I decide to aid you or not."

"Of course," Faln said, bowing deeply. "Your authority is, as always, unchallenged in this land."

Kaa snorted, and the sudden breath of foul air made Faln choke. "Flattery is foolish, mortal. Demons such as I have no use for it, except to use it on your pitiful species. Besides, it is unnecessary. Fortunately for you, I have already chosen to do the plan you called me for. I sensed the children the moment they arrived in Meynch. But..." Kaa paused, "who is the one who will be our Judas?"

Judge Faln looked curious.

Kaa laughed and shook the rafters. "Never mind. I forgot that you would not understand the meaning. Who will betray the children?"

Faln told Kaa what he had planned.

"Well, well, well. I must say, mortal, I have not seen your breed of shrewdness in many centuries. The Enemy thinks that families are the closest bond. Ha! Of all the bonds to break, it is the easiest. I merely plant a seed of rebellion in a child's heart, encourage a roving eye in a husband, fester discontentment in a wife's heart, and very quickly family loyalty becomes a thing of the past. I am pleased, Faln. Pleased just enough to spare your miserable life in spite of your arrogance. You will serve my purpose well enough. Another child shall betray the Children of Prophecy."

"It shouldn't have been that easy," Abi said to Nathan.

Nathan and Abi were sitting on a fallen log, watching the colorful sunset light up the sky and the scenic forest as it prepared for the night. The magic of the seemingly enchanted scenery mixed with Nathan's nearness gave Abi a giddy feeling. But it subsided when she thought of the reason they were there—taking shelter as they ran from powers they had never known existed.

They had stopped at Kes's house for food and supplies, but they were hurried, fearing the danger was not past. They packed a small cloth backpack with enough food and water for several days, but when it ran out… Abi shuddered. She didn't want to think of that. Kes had told them about a place they could seek refuge—but not for very long.

Around an hour later, they had reached the dense woods a mile away from the town, and Nathan and Chris agreed this was far enough for that day. Chris had gone to look for wood to make a campfire while Abi and Nathan prepared a makeshift bed made out of grass and sticks for Weana, who was already half asleep. After ten minutes, Chris was still gone, and Weana had since fallen asleep, leaving Abi and Nathan alone with the trees and their own thoughts.

"It wasn't. Judge Faln, for some reason, *wanted* us to go. There should have been guards and such, but there weren't. He probably told them to go. And even though he said you'd have to leave me, he's not dumb. He knew you would try to help me. What I don't understand is why." He paused. "He's still going to declare us outlaws, you know."

"We aren't technically outlaws. Judge Faln said we were free to go, remember?" Abi replied.

"Doesn't matter. He'll find some sort of loophole, probably that he didn't say I was free to go. No matter what else he is planning, I know he wants us all to be outlaws, so that he can do whatever he wants to us and still not be technically breaking the law."

"Don't forget Weana." Abi said innocently. At the mention of Weana's name, dark suspicions rose up in Nathan's mind. *Why did Judge Faln wink at her as he left? Why did he say we were more beneficial free than locked up? Did she agree to something? Is that why Kes and Marla are still in prison?*

But Nathan pushed them aside for now and sighed. Putting an arm around Abi's waist, Nathan asked, "If you had known that all of this would happen, would you have still come to Meynch?"

Abi sighed. "That's like asking Lucy if she would have still opened the wardrobe if she had known about the battle with the White Witch or asking Frodo if he would have still taken the One Ring to Mount Doom if he had understood completely what he would have to go through to get there." Seeing Nathan's mystified expression, she laughed softly.

"I'm sorry. I keep forgetting that you don't know the books in my world. The point is, I don't think that was ever my decision to make. A higher power guided me here."

"The King?"

"I don't know. But I think we'll find out."

Morning came swiftly to the children in the woods, but they were prepared. Everything they needed was in their backpack, and Chris carefully covered the smoldering embers of their campfire with grass and dirt. Abi and Nathan did their part by picking more berries from the bushes around them to eat later. But Weana just stood, digging her shoe in the soil.

"All right, I think we're good," Chris said after thoroughly examining the area. "This place looks like no one's been here."

"And just in time!" As Abi spoke, bright rays of the emerging sun peeked through the dense vegetation and lit up their alcove. "Let's go!"

Chris held Weana's hand, and Nathan held out his to Abi. She took it hesitantly, and he saw her shiver slightly though there was a warm breeze. He looked at her wide, trusting, jade eyes and asked, "Did your Lucy and Frodo succeed?"

She nodded. "But it's just a story. This is real."

"There is no such thing as *just* a story. A story was never meant to end with the book. It was made to live on in your actions and reactions. It was meant to inspire us by showing us true courage and goodness in spite of their flaws. It was meant to make us want to be better people and give us a longing for our own happy ending."

Abi was taken aback by Nathan's eloquence. "Wow. That was so deep. I had no idea guys even thought about stuff like that. I know the guys in my world don't."

He grinned and squeezed her hand gently. "Come on. We have a long way to go."

Meeting the Stranger's Friends

Farther into the woods, Abi saw a small cottage that looked abandoned and quickly pointed it out to Chris. Vines were growing over the walls, and the door and windows barely hung on their hinges.

"Come on! This is the place Kes told us about." Chris motioned to Nathan and Weana.

The cottage sat at the top on a high grassy mound, and the many steps to the front door spiraled around the hill. Abi was exhausted just looking at it. "We have to climb *that*?"

Chris grinned. "You never know when you're going to need to be in shape. You should've participated in PE instead of standing on the side and talking with Sarah."

Abi rolled her eyes. "Whatever."

Finally, after a long and very tiring climb, they reached the top. Chris lifted his hand to knock, but Nathan held him back. "Let me do it. He knows me."

Chris nodded and moved aside. Nathan knocked and waited for someone to answer.

After a few minutes, a hoarse, dry voice responded. "Is that ye, Mother?"

"The ultimate sacrifice—the lamb gave up its crown to die so I can live," Nathan replied. He mouthed,

"It's a password," to Abi and Chris, whose eyebrows were raised.

The door immediately opened, and a thin, old man with mesmerizing dark eyes peered at them. He nodded then motioned them in.

Once they stepped inside the door, they had the strangest sensation of plunging downward like in a elevator, but the feeling came and went so quickly that Abi wondered if she had just imagined it.

Abi and Chris looked around. The house seemed to be bigger on the inside than on the outside. The room they were in was huge, but she noticed that the floor, even though it almost looked like a hardwood floor, was thick, dry mud. There was a large, rough-looking wooden table in the middle of the room with nine chairs. There was a closet door on three of the four walls around them, but there was no door on the wall behind them.

Nathan talked with their host in hushed voices. Weana, without looking at anything or anyone, went to the opposite corner of the room and sat down, bringing her knees up and hiding her face in her lap. Abi and Chris sat down, facing each other at the table.

Eventually, Nathan and the older man walked over, and Nathan sat next to Abi. "It's all right. I explained our situation and he said we can stay a while."

Their host pulled out a chair at the head of the table when a loud knock interrupted him. "Excuse me, children." He walked over to the square and disappeared.

"Whoa!" Chris exclaimed. "Where did he go?"

"He just went upstairs," Nathan replied.

"What about the whole 'stairs' part? I mean, you guys don't have glass elevators right?"

"I'm not sure what a glass ele-vator is, but no, this house doesn't use stairs. It's…hard to explain. You stand on the upstairs square, the square gives out, and you drop down to the lower level of the house. But if you stand on the downstairs square, it almost bounces you to the ground level above." Nathan used his hands to draw a picture in the air of what he was saying. "It's a strange invention. I don't completely understand it myself."

"So, it's like an elevator and a trampoline combined." Chris was trying to get a mental image and not quite succeeding.

Nathan shrugged, but Abi nodded. "That sounds right. Wow, that would be a really cool thing to have back home! We should go invent it!" Abi laughed. "Tired of climbing stairs? Then try our invention: The Trampoline-vator!"

They heard a whoosh, and their host appeared in the square. He sat down at the head of the table, carrying a rolled up piece of parchment in his hand.

Nathan stood up. "Abi, Chris, this is Seginus, a wise and respected man in the community—until he became friends with the Stranger. Now he is respected among the friends of the Stranger, but unfortunately the lawmen have branded him an outlaw and forgotten his wise teachings." Nathan made the introductions quickly, but out of the corner of his eye he saw Abi frown and tap her chin with her index finger.

The old man nodded. "It's a pleasure to meet the children that have the lawmen so riled. Very few have the courage to attempt to thwart their plans. But I'm afraid your friend Nathan is too generous. Even before the Stranger came, not many listened to me."

Suddenly Abi lit up. "Seginus! You're the one I saw!"

"We've met? Oh, it's a sure sign that I'm getting old when I can't remember—"

"No, no, I mean I had a vision. A guy named Jonathan was having a meeting with some other guys, and you came. You and Jonathan joked around, and he was kind of making fun of your age. You told Jonathan that you were suspicious of Micah, but you weren't sure. He actually *is* a high-ranking lawman, by the way. And you said a prophecy that I saw in another vision—something about children…" Abi paused partly because everyone was staring at her and partly because something just occurred to her. "We're the children!"

"Astounding!" Seginus leaned forward. "A child who has visions! Such a thing has never been heard of before. This is more indisputable proof that you are the children of prophecy." He chuckled. "As for the informal manner between Jonathan and me, he is the only one who can address me that way, because I am his adoptive father. His parents died when he had only seen five summers, and I found him at the door of the courthouse with nary a note or any hint of where he was from. To the best of my ability, I instilled in him devotion to the Shepherd King and a solid moral code, and when I accepted the Stranger's teachings, he did as well, not because I told him to, but because he felt the truth of the Stranger's words in his own heart."

But Seginus suddenly sank back into his chair. "Micah is a high-ranking lawman, you say? I'm not completely surprised. I suspected something wasn't right about him. I should have seen it, but I tried to ignore the signs at first. There are so many lawmen; I suppose I hoped that one of the lower, petty ones was the spy, someone that had not once been my friend," he looked at Abi and Chris, "as well as a friend of your father's, according to Nathan. I've no doubt that he's been keeping Judge Faln up to date on our every move…the black-hearted, miserable traitor. What's surprising is that they haven't arrested anyone based on all that information. I have to wonder what they're waiting for."

A knock on the door startled them. Abi gasped. "D-d-do you think that's them?"

Seginus stood up slowly. "Interesting timing." He looked at the nervous faces at the table. "I'll go answer the door. If it's lawmen, Nathan, you know what to do."

"Yes, sir."

Seginus walked to a large square drawn in the floor, stepped on it, and suddenly disappeared.

Nathan immediately took charge. "Okay, Abi, go to the room on your left. Chris, go with her. I'll go to the room on the right with Weana." Abi and Chris nodded and hurried through the doorway. Weana would not look up, so Nathan grabbed her hand and led her toward the other door.

But before they could all reach safety, two men and Seginus appeared in the square with a loud whoosh.

"An underground home, eh? Seginus, you are clever." A broad-shouldered man with long, wavy, red hair chuckled.

Abi turned around and gasped. "Jonathan!"

"Have we met?" Jonathan looked at her curiously.

"My friends, let me introduce you to the children of prophecy. This is Abi," Abi extended her hand toward him to shake, but instead he pecked it lightly. *Did he just kiss my hand? Oh my gosh, it's like the medieval times!* She blushed, "and her brother Chris." Chris stepped beside Abi and bowed.

"Children, apparently you know Jonathan, but this is Aaren." Seginus pointed to the other man who was tall and slender with short sandy, red hair and bright, golden-brown eyes.

Jonathan bowed. "We greet you in the name of the King and as fellow strangers in this world."

"Are you from another world too?" Abi asked.

"No, it's not because we are from another world like you," Jonathan rushed to explain, "but because the Stranger's words about the King's Castle made us feel like strangers in Meynch. We could no longer settle for the mediocre pleasures of Meynch, but longed for the richer joy that comes in the presence of the Shepherd King."

"Jonathan, sir, we haven't met, but…" Abi started to explain to Jonathan why she had recognized him.

"She has visions," Seginus interrupted.

"Oh?" Jonathan raised an eyebrow.

"Yes, sir, and I saw you and some of the other strangers in one of them."

Seginus turned to Nathan and Weana, who stood gaping at them. "So sorry for worrying you. This old mind quickly forgot that we were having company. Jonathan was the one who sent me this message," he held up the parchment in his hand, "saying he was on his way. Sit down, gentlemen. You, too, children. We can all trade stories soon, but first I have some bad news."

Jonathan nodded. "We do, too. Someone has betrayed us! During our meeting this morning, the lawmen stormed in and attempted to arrest us. Fortunately, many of us managed to escape, because the lawmen did not have enough forces to subdue all of us. I believe the lawmen did not realize how many of us there were, since we had disguised our true numbers by separating into different houses across Meynch for most of our previous meetings. However, they did recognize who we are, and now we are all in grave danger."

Seginus looked at him sadly. "The betrayer is Micah. This child, Abi…" Seginus motioned to Abi, "…told me that Micah has been conspiring with Judge Faln all along. What's done is done, though. All we can do now is be cautious, and follow the Stranger's advice: be as wise as serpents, and as innocent as doves. However, there has been an additional complication. The children have twice escaped the lawmen, and they are probably more than a little unhappy. If they discover we are harboring them, it will give them the excuse they need to arrest us all. We need to—"

"We didn't escape the lawmen the second time. Faln let us go," Chris interrupted.

Everyone stared at him, wide-eyed. Chris tugged at the collar of his shirt nervously. "Uh…"

Jonathan began to explain. "The lawmen have a bad habit of letting prisoners suspected of illegal activity go free and sending something to watch them."

"But we didn't see anyone." Abi looked around nervously. Her eyes rested on Weana, who was looking down at her lap.

"It's not something you can *see* necessarily. The Stranger told us about it. It's a spirit, an evil spirit, that follows you. But I don't think you and your brother have one." Jonathan looked pointedly at Nathan and Weana, the latter which would not meet his eyes, and Abi clearly heard what he *wasn't* saying.

Suddenly all the lamps in the room flickered then dimmed. The remaining light cast eerie shadows on the walls.

Abi, frightened, reached for Chris's hand. *They're just shadows. They're not alive.* Abi repeated this to herself as she fearfully watched the sinister dark mass spread throughout the room.

Gradually, Abi became aware of a delightful feeling that spread from her head to the tips of her toes. Feeling tingly and comfortably warm, she relaxed unconsciously, allowing herself to be immersed in the curious sensation of being completely secure and happy for the first time in a long while. The shadows became nothing but a distant memory in the face of this overwhelming love and peace washing over her.

"Abi!" Chris murmured softly, startling Abi out of her serenity. "You're glowing!"

A Victim of Evil

"I am?" Abi looked down at her body. She couldn't see any light. "What are you talking about? I'm not glowing." She looked up at Chris. *He* was shining brightly! "But you are!"

"Are not!"

"Are, too!"

"Are not!"

"Guys!" Nathan's voice interrupted their argument. "You *both* are glowing!"

They looked toward the sound of Nathan's voice. They could see his outline, and it was also radiant!

"What's going on?"

"We're *all* glowing!" said Jonathan after looking around the table.

"Except me," a small voice said. Abi recognized it as Weana's voice and turned toward it. Weana was right. There was no light around her at all. If anything, the shadows seemed darker and thicker around her. She got up and moved to a far corner of the room.

All of a sudden, a voice resonated through the room. Majestic, powerful, tender, loving, and compassionate all at once, it inspired fear and awe in them all.

"Do not fear, for I am with you. My presence surrounds you. No evil can penetrate as long as you have faith in me."

Something inside Abi instinctively responded to that voice and made her want to sing for joy and bow with her face to the ground. *The Shepherd King! He's making us glow! But how? Is this some sort of magic?*

The shadows, in response to the King's words, seemed to grow darker and creep closer to the group. But just like the voice had said, the shadows could only come so close before they were barred by the golden glow that surrounded Abi, Chris, Nathan, Seginus, Jonathan, and Aaren.

Abi glanced toward the square on the other side of the room. She blinked, being startled. She *knew* she would have heard someone coming, yet a sinister, ghostly figure stood against the backdrop of shadows, its long cloak glowing violet. It wore a broad fedora that covered its eyes, yet Abi could feel it staring at her. She shivered.

"Chris!" she whispered anxiously.

"What?"

"There's a creepy *thing* in the square." She pointed toward the being.

Chris followed Abi's finger with his eyes. "Reilim, lord of the shadows," he whispered.

"What?"

Chris looked startled by his own words and looked at Abi. "Don't ask me how I knew that. It just…came out." His gaze swung back to the being. "Whatever that is, it means trouble."

The unearthly phantom moved, or glided, closer to Weana. Abi and Chris saw it stretch out its pale hands to hover over her head.

"Weana, look out!" Abi stood up, forgetting the eerie shadows for a moment, and ran to Weana. When she didn't receive a response, she shook Weana's shoulders. "Weana, come on!" She attempted to grab her hand to pull her away from the specter.

Suddenly, Weana lifted her head to look her in the eye, and Abi stepped back, shocked. The wide, long-lashed, blue-gray eyes that had once held innocence and love looked back at her with an infinite malice and bitterness that was nursed for centuries in darkness and blood.

"You aren't Weana," Abi whispered.

There was no need for a response. Both of them knew the truth.

The dark phantom surrounded Weana, and she, along with all the shadows and the phantom, disappeared. The lights flickered back to life, lighting the room but not completely banishing the sinister mood that still hung in the air.

A Prophetic Mission

Abi backed up slowly and ran into Jonathan's solid chest. Though no one else but Chris and Abi could see the phantom, Chris jumped into action as Abi tried to help Weana. "Jonathan, sir, Aaren, come on!"

Without questioning, for they *could* see the encroaching darkness surrounding Abi and Weana, the men leaped to their feet and pulled out their swords to come to her aid.

Some of the shadows attempted to form a wall separating them from her, but Aaren and Jonathan cut through the murky barrier.

Jonathan's hazel eyes gleamed with compassion and sadness. "I'm sorry," he murmured.

She buried her face in Jonathan's tunic. The tears threatening to spill down her face reminded her, as no sermon could, of Weana's lost innocence and of the part she had played in Weana's bitterness. Jonathan enfolded her in a warm embrace, and Abi felt him awkwardly pat her back.

When Abi finally pulled away, she felt dazed, feeling in her gut that she had forgotten something very important.

Suddenly she realized what Judge Faln had said. Her father, uncle, and aunt would "stay with him for a little while longer." But for what reason? And what would he do to them in the meantime?

"We have to rescue them!" At the puzzled looks directed her way, she covered her mouth. Had she finished her thoughts out loud?

"Who?" Chris asked.

"My father! Kes and Marla! We've been here safe and sound while they've been stuck in a dungeon with Judge Faln, and who knows what he's done to them!" Abi, ashamed, took the cloth Seginus now offered her and hurriedly wiped her eyes.

Nathan hit his forehead with the palm of his hand. "You're right! In all the rush, I never stopped to ask why Judge Faln kept them! I can't believe I completely forgot about them! I feel awful."

Jonathan and the other Strangers watched, bewildered, as the teens began to devise a plan. A few minutes later, Seginus, who had been carefully listening and had grasped the situation, interrupted, saying sadly, "Children, there is no way you can get them out in your own power."

Abi, Chris, and Nathan turned to him. "Well, then, what are we supposed to do?" Nathan asked angrily.

"What you were supposed to do in the first place. Find the Stranger. You must understand what he taught, and you must submit to the Shepherd King."

"But haven't we been..." Abi paused. Had they really been searching for the Stranger? Maybe in the beginning, but soon they had gotten so caught up in everything else that they had forgotten their main purpose—to find the Stranger and go back to Earth.

"You still have a long journey ahead of you," Seginus continued. "Now that you have realized the existence of the unearthly influences in Meynch, you will see everything and everyone here in a new light. But for you to get home, and for your father to be freed, and for Weana to be released of the dark spirit that holds her, you *must* find the Stranger."

"What about me and Kes and Marla?" Nathan asked.

Seginus turned his head to look at him. "There's no prophecy about you, so I suggest just staying here." He turned back to Abi and Chris and handed them a map. "This is a map of Meynch. Just a word of warning, we share our eastern border, the mountains of Troche, with another town. They don't exactly like us, so I suggest you don't cross the mountains.

"Now, children, step on the square." Seginus motioned to the square on the other side of the room where they had first entered.

The minute they stepped in it, they disappeared.

Abi and Chris found themselves on Seginus's front porch, staring at the old, creaking house they had thought was his home. They looked at each other and grinned.

"I can't believe we were actually hiding out underground!" Abi said. "That sounds so medieval or like the first century Christians during Nero's reign."

"Except for the whole trampoline-vator thing." Chris grinned. "That was so weird. How *does* Seginus do that, anyway?"

Abi shrugged. "Maybe one day we can ask him. Right now, we have work to do. How long has it been?"

Chris looked at his bare wrist, then sheepishly shrugged and squinted at the sun. "I think it's almost noon, so we've been in there at least a couple of hours. But it seemed like days!"

"I don't think time is normal here. I had a vision yesterday that it had only been ten minutes back home since we came to Meynch, and that was after we spent a whole day here."

"That makes sense. I mean, in all the stories, it's the same way." Chris crossed his arms and looked at his sister. "So what do we do now? I mean, how are we going to find the Stranger?"

"Well, let's think about this. Didn't the Stranger say he was the King's son? And my vision said that the King's castle is at the top of the mountains of Troche. So let's start by going there."

Unrolling the map in his hands, Chris studied it carefully. "Okay. According to the map, the mountains of Troche are…that way." He pointed deeper into the forest. "On the other side of the woods."

"Now we're getting somewhere! Let's go!" Abi took one last glance at the vine-grown cottage, then followed Chris into the forest.

Mysterious visions, ancient prophecies, explosive secrets, she contemplated. *I feel like I traded places with Lucy Pevensie. All my daydreams of adventure are coming to life, and I'm totally overwhelmed. It's not like I'm one of those kids who are always up for excitement. I much prefer sitting on my couch with a good book and just reading about these kinds of adventures. I'm not cut out for all the constantly-eluding-danger adventure stuff. I'm not a fantasy heroine. I just hope the King knew what he was doing when he picked us.*

"So what do we do?" Jonathan's voice rang out in the silence that had descended over the room after Abi and Chris had left. "What can we do to help them?"

Seginus nodded. "Your willingness to help is not only welcome, but essential. Your mission, along with Nathan, is to rescue Kes, Marla, and Weana. I knew Nathan would need some help."

At the mention of his name, Nathan turned to face them. "I'm sorry, Jonathan, Aaren. I don't know you very well. But I do know that Seginus trusts you, and that's good enough for me. I do need all the help I can get. But we have to hurry! Who knows what Judge Faln has done to them already?"

Aaren had not said anything since they had arrived. Apparently, he was the strong, silent sort and was used to letting Jonathan do all the talking. But now he looked as if he were about to say something and was restraining himself.

Seginus and Jonathan waited expectantly. The silence was oppressive.

Finally, Aaren could take it no longer.

"How are we going to do that? Judge Faln is probably keeping them under tight lock and key. There is no way they can escape, nor can we get them free!"

"Remember what the Stranger told us? The King knows every situation. He will provide a way for us to rescue them." Seginus spoke confidently, apparently believing it with his whole heart.

"But what about the children's father?" Jonathan asked.

As if in response, the Voice that had promised them protection from the shadows earlier resonated through the room again. "Scott has been summoned back to his own world. His work is done for now. The children must find me on their own, and eventually they will gain faith in the Shepherd King and His Son."

"So how do we do that?" Nathan echoed Aaren's original question. He wasn't sure whether Seginus or the mysterious Voice would answer.

There was no response from the Voice, but Seginus commented slyly, "Actually, I do have a plan. Even though I'm not sure all of you will like it, I'm sure it will work." His blue eyes, seemingly brightened with ageless wisdom, now twinkled merrily as he looked at Nathan. Nathan gulped nervously.

"Nathan, come out! I promise you it's not that bad," Seginus called. He stood leaning against the wall that faced the room Nathan had gone in to prepare for his role in Kes and Marla's escape. The boy had complained, begged, and yelled against his part in the jailbreak, but Seginus had turned a deaf ear. "You're the only one young enough," he had said. And so, eventually, Nathan reluctantly cooperated.

"This is embarrassing," Nathan mumbled. The door slowly opened, and Seginus attempted to stifle a grin, knowing how much it cost Nathan to do this, but his eyes sparkled.

Nathan was dressed in a long, flowing, silk dress that was embroidered with delicate flowers. His muscular frame had been bound to look as if he had a girlish figure, and the high lace collar covered cuts on his freshly shaven face, not that there was much to shave in the first place, much to Nathan's chagrin. A thin, gold circlet rested on his brow, and he wore a wig of long, brown curls. His glowering eyes, however, refused to match the image he was supposed to portray.

"I'm glad you find this amusing, Seginus," Nathan grumbled. "Remind me again, how is humiliating me by making me look like a girl, a princess no less, going to help Kes, Marla, and Weana escape?" Nathan asked for the tenth time since he had been told of Seginus's plan.

Seginus eyes gleamed with suppressed mirth, but he answered patiently. "You, along with Jonathan and Aaren, who will pose as your bodyguards, will go to the courthouse. You as a foreign princess will make up a story about how you need more companions, and you heard they had some available. They will, of course, say they do not, but you will tell them some story about how, in your country, you use prisoners as slaves to the royalty. You're going to have to be creative and believable.

"Assuming that part of the plan goes off without a hitch, they will probably show you the dungeons and ask you to take your pick. Judge Faln will probably not let you pick Kes, Marla, and Weana, but you will see where they are. After a thorough examination, you will pronounce them all unsuitable. You will stay at the courthouse for a few more hours with the excuse that you cannot leave without your bodyguards and they were still doing an errand you sent them to do.

"This is where Jonathan and Aaren come in. They will offer the guards glasses of water filled with an odorless, tasteless drug that will knock them out instantly and slip the keys out of the guards' belt. They then will make a quick imprint of them in a tablet made out of wet clay and report back to you. By then, the drug will have worn off, and all the guards will remember is drinking a glass of water. They will not remember Jonathan or Aaren.

"Jonathan and Aaren will take the imprinted clay tablet to a smith named Contrand. He will forge a key into the clay mold, and they will bring the key to you. You will pretend to need another tour, discreetly slip Kes the key, and leave quickly. Kes and Marla will know not to use the key immediately. It will probably be a couple of hours before they will attempt a jailbreak."

Nathan crossed his arms and glowered. "This whole plan is so ridiculously complicated. Couldn't I just be a foreign *prince*?"

"As any lawmen knows, according to the law of the King, they are to respect ladies. They are more likely to do as you ask."

"More likely? That's not very certain. Seginus, I'm not sure about this. Isn't this lying? The law of the King tells us not to lie." Nathan was using every argument he could. But Seginus had a swift retort ready.

"No. You will not *say* you are a foreign princess, but you will act like one. The lawmen will assume you are what you act like even though they do not live up to that standard themselves. You *do* need Kes, Marla, and Weana's companionship, and Jonathan and Aaren *are* protecting you. I admit, this is not completely honest, but I am sure the King will pardon our methods."

Nathan huffed just as Jonathan and Aaren emerged from another room. They were dressed in suits of armor, and low helmets covered their eyes. Swords hung at their sides. Nathan did not recognize the coat of arms but supposed it was meaningless except as a way to prove he was from another kingdom.

When they saw Nathan, Jonathan shook the room with a booming guffaw. "Nathan, I know this is for a good cause, but I just can't take you seriously in that getup. I think it would be best that, if this succeeds, we'll keep the details between us."

Nathan blushed. "Thank you, sir." His mind went back to the first time he had seen Jonathan and Aaren. It seemed every time he saw them, he got the same reaction from them…

George and Christina Laurel stood in a large crowd that had gathered on the outskirts of town. It seemed everywhere the Stranger went, the crowd followed him. They had brought their only child, Nathan, along partly because the twelve-year old boy was getting curious about why they had begun to return home late, when work hours ended early in the afternoon, and partly because they didn't want to leave him at home alone. Odd things had been happening ever since the Stranger had arrived, and they weren't taking any chances.

"The King loves you very much, and He cares about everything in your life. Just because you can't hear Him or see Him anymore, doesn't mean He has abandoned you…"

Nathan was a bright boy and quickly realized this man was not a lawman attempting to draw attention in the streets. He didn't emphasize the laws of the King or even His coming judgment; instead, he told of the King's love and compassion.

Almost as if reading his thoughts, Christina bent to whisper in her son's ear, "That's the Stranger, honey."

The Stranger!

Nathan had always wanted to serve the King. The lawmen said the only way to serve the King was to be a lawman, and so he put his heart in his studies of the law.

But secretly he had hoped serving the King was more than that. The Stranger claimed to be the Son of the King. Maybe he knew if there was more to serving the King than dusty, old laws.

On that reasoning, he slipped out of the relaxed hold of his parents, who were absorbed in the Stranger's teaching, and weaved his way through the crowd closer to the Stranger.

Suddenly, two hands grabbed his shoulders and held him back. He twisted to see a young man that had probably seen no more than twenty summers yet. He had a full, red beard that matched his fiery hair. "What are you doing, boy?" the man asked gruffly.

Nathan felt slightly embarrassed as the man looked at Nathan like he was a bothersome fly, but he answered with more bravado than he felt. "I want to ask the Stranger a question!"

"Can't you see he's busy teaching?"

"But…"

"Maybe later, kiddo." Another man with short, sandy, red hair and bright, golden-brown eyes joined the conversation. "The Stranger's a busy man."

Nathan turned away, dejected. *I hate being a kid! No one takes me seriously!*

"Don't turn away the children. Aren't they the heirs of the kingdom?" The Stranger stood a few feet away, looking at Nathan kindly, and beckoned for him to come closer.

Nathan shyly approached the Stranger as the men stepped aside and the crowd parted, giving him a clear path.

The Stranger smiled, not a condescending smirk like the lawmen, but like he had been waiting for this moment for a long time. It warmed Nathan and gave him courage. "Now what did you want to ask me?"

Nathan bowed respectfully as was proper for a young man to an elder and murmured quietly, "I should like to serve the King, but I don't know how."

The Stranger beamed now. "So you shall." Then he turned to some other men who were badgering him with questions. Nathan felt abruptly ignored, and, being surprised, he was pushed out of the way by people eager to talk to the Stranger just as he had done.

"Nathan!"

I never told him my name, Nathan thought.

But he heard the unspoken command, and he obediently pushed his way through the crowd to the Stranger again.

Once he reached him, he realized that his parents had come to stand beside the Stranger. Why'd he have to get Mom and Dad involved? It was just a question!

"Nathan, after you finish your apprenticeship to Kes, you will study under Jonathan and Aaren." The Stranger pointed to the two men that had stopped Nathan earlier. "You will learn more about the King and this town, though, from two children that are… very different from you, and they will change this town forever." He smiled mysteriously.

Then he disappeared.

Nathan smiled at the memory, but suddenly he gasped, drawing Seginus's attention. "The Stranger knew about Abi and Chris!" he exclaimed.

Seginus stared at him then began to smile. "My boy, the Stranger knows everything."

"But how—"

"No time to analyze that now. We must hurry. The lives of our friends hang in the balance."

A Reunion and a Reminder

The strategy was put into action that evening. Everything went according to plan. The lawmen fell for Nathan's disguise but not before, to Nathan's increasing humiliation, he had to act dainty and flirtatious, flattering the lawmen with the most insincere compliments. It did not hurt that Aaren had written an official-looking document for Nathan from "her father, King Karl," that basically threatened any who disobey his "daughter." Their plan was infallible, until…

"What do you mean, Contrand's not here?" Jonathan exclaimed.

He and Aaren had drugged the guards and imprinted their keys in the tablet. They had immediately set off to Contrand's blacksmith shop, eager to get the key. But the smirking, skinny man looked at them like they were dirt on his shoes and refused to tell them where Contrand was.

"I'm telling you, I own this joint, and I've owned it for months. The guy I bought it from didn't say his name and left with a couple of men and didn't say when he would be back or where he was going." The man was obviously enjoying their frustration.

Aaren had been closely analyzing the man, and he motioned Jonathan aside.

"That man is lying through his teeth. His eyes are greedy, and he won't look you in the eye when he talks. I'd bet good money that either he's working with the lawmen and they have him, or that this man's a thief and Contrand's a captive in his own house."

Jonathan nodded. "I've got a good way to find out."

"Sir," Aaren said minutes later in a honeyed voice, "we haven't had the pleasure of knowing your name."

"My name," the man replied just as smoothly, "is obvious to those with clear eyes."

Jonathan squinted at him. His shirt, he now noticed, was odd. It looked like it was backward…

Suddenly Jonathan knew who it was.

"Titus, you old rascal! I thought you were dead!"

Titus, for it was indeed he, peered at them closely. "Do I know you?"

"Yes, you do, but let me remind you how we last met. As I recall, it was quite an eventful day in your life…"

Jonathan rubbed his feet discreetly. He had been walking too long, and his feet complained with every step. But the Stranger aimed to reach the center of town by high sun, so Jonathan picked up the pace, not wanting to be left behind as it was already awhile past breakfast.

They had been in the far outskirts of Meynch, and the Stranger, at dawn, had woken them with the instruction to meet him at the main road to journey back to town. They had been walking all morning.

Suddenly the Stranger stopped. A blind man sat in the middle of the road, not completely blocking the path but hindering any group more than two people walking side by side, which was obviously them.

"Coins, coins for a blind man!" he called halfheartedly. He obviously wasn't expecting anyone to stop for him.

The Stranger approached the beggar and touched his shoulder.

"I thought he wanted us to hurry," Jonathan mumbled to himself and then felt ashamed for his callous words. *The man obviously needs more help than we can give. Maybe the Stranger will just give him some money.*

"Huh?" The man looked up with sightless eyes. "Do you have money?"

"What is your name?" The Stranger's voice was infinitely gentle.

"Titus, kind sir."

"What do you want most in the world?"

The Stranger's question apparently struck the man as odd, for his face grew puzzled, but he answered, "My sight, sir, so I can see my wife and baby girl. But 'tis an impossible hope. All the healers have said my sight cannot be restored. It would take a miracle."

If only you knew how many miracles I've seen in this past week, Jonathan thought. *The Stranger has great power, more than any man alive.*

"Stand up." The Stranger held out his hand, and the man groped for it and unsteadily rose to his feet. "Touch your eyes."

Titus touched his eyes with the hand the Stranger had held. He blinked, and Jonathan stared. His eyes were as blue as a cloudless summer sky.

"I can see!" Titus exclaimed.

Murmurs spread through the group, and all eyes looked at the Stranger. He had a delighted smile on his face as if he was looking at a beautiful painting being unveiled or a colorful bird unfold its wings.

Others were not so joyfully accepting. "I don't believe it." A big, brown-haired man stepped forward from the crowd. "Sir," the man addressed Titus, "how many fingers am I holding up?" He held up three fingers.

"Three," the beggar confidently replied without a moment's hesitation.

"This is a trick!" someone shouted.

"I've known this man for years! He's been blind since birth, but now he can see!"

"How did the Stranger do it?"

"It's not a trick! I've been blind since I first entered the world, but this man has restored my sight! I can see for myself all the things people have only described to me. I can see those trees, I can see those flowers, and I can see those clouds..." The beggar danced around the path, reveling in the little things that he could now enjoy.

Two muscular men stepped out of the crowd and grabbed Titus's arms while he was rejoicing in his newfound sight. "You're coming with us, sir." Everyone knew this man would be questioned and interrogated by the lawmen since they were obviously lawmen police, but no one moved as the struggling beggar was taken to his certain doom.

"Never forget," Jonathan whispered as Titus was dragged by him. His head turned, and he stared at Jonathan.

"I won't," the previously blind beggar mouthed. "I won't."

"Apparently you have, though," Jonathan finished sadly.

"No I haven't! Every time I see the glorious sunrise, I thank the King for sending the Stranger to heal me. He has truly blessed me."

Aaren grunted. "I don't think the King would be very pleased with how you chose to use his blessing. Neither, I would imagine, are your wife and child."

Titus's voice grew bitter. "My wife left me, and took our baby girl with her, soon after the lawmen released me. She couldn't handle the scandal, I guess. I haven't heard from her since." His voice broke, and he cleared his throat. "As for my line of work, that isn't my fault! A man has to earn a living somehow. The lawmen threatened to kill me because I defended the Stranger when they interrogated me all those years ago. That destroys my chances of ever seeking a job there—"Jonathan raised an eyebrow."—not that I'd ever want to," Titus quickly corrected. "It's too late for me to learn a craft, so what does that leave me?" Titus slammed his fist on the table. "Nothing!"

"Your situation is a hard one, I admit. And we are not here to condemn you and your choices. That is between you and the King," Jonathan said, not unkindly. "But I *am* asking you, for the sake of the Stranger who healed you, to tell us where Contrand is."

Titus stroked his chin with one long, bony finger, his face wrinkled in indecision. "You have backed me into a corner. I must honor your request for the sake of the Stranger, as you said, but I place what I have earned in jeopardy if I do."

"I know you will do the right thing." Jonathan nodded confidently though his emotions teetered between hope and expectation of disappointment. Their entire plan to rescue Kes and his family rested on Titus's decision.

Titus visibly struggled for a moment, then relented. "Very well. Come with me."

Titus motioned for them to follow him through the shop. Jonathan and Aaren breathed a collective sigh of relief and walked forward. Jonathan ducked under a low-hanging leather saddle, but Aaren was distracted by the beautiful silver plates and got a bruise on his forehead.

Eventually they reached the back rooms, and Titus opened the door. A big man with dark hair that was peppered with gray was tied to a wooden chair. He was gagged, but when he saw Jonathan and Aaren, his eyes widened. He struggled to free himself, but his hands were tied tightly behind his back and his legs to the legs of the chair, so he only succeeded in making the chair bounce up and down.

Aaren went immediately to help untie the man, but Jonathan stifled a grin at Contrand's predicament. This was the man who used to be the rough teenager who beat up boys after school instead of using healthier outlets for all the power inside of him. Despite the fact that the Stranger had through much effort turned him from his violent ways and redirected his passion to defending the King, Contrand still retained most of his brute strength. The thought of Titus overcoming Contrand and putting him in this position was rather amusing.

Jonathan sobered, though, when he remembered the reason for their coming and went to help Aaren untie him.

The minute they loosened the gag, Contrand spat it out like it was poison. "Thank the King you have come! This common thief took over my shop two days ago!" He glared at Titus who held up his hands in mock surrender and smirked.

"I have a score to settle with him," Contrand said as he stood and cracked his knuckles loudly. "But first, why have you now decided to make a long-overdue visit?"

Jonathan and Aaren quickly explained the situation, and Contrand agreed to forge the key and began at once. While he worked, Jonathan, Aaren, and Titus talked about the Stranger.

"Remember when he told the story of the servant who owed the King hundreds of dollars and was forgiven..." Aaren began.

"…but the man turned around and didn't forgive his friend who owed him fifty cents." Titus nodded. "I felt particularly convicted after that. The Stranger was a master at making his point through the use of a seemingly simple story."

"Remember when the lawmen brought a man caught stealing gold from the courthouse treasury and asked him to break the man's hand?" Jonathan asked. "The Stranger knew the punishment for stealing was the loss of a hand, and the lawmen knew if he agreed, he would be contradicting everything he had said about the King's love and mercy…"

"…but if he refused, he would be basically pronouncing his death sentence. So the Stranger avoided their trap by asking the man who was without sin to break the man's hand. No one could, of course."

Aaren hesitated, then asked slowly, "Remember when Arana and Kristi's brother died?"

The conversation paused. Arana and Kristi were sisters and close family friends of Jonathan. Their brother, Nicholas, was a righteous man who worked hard and loved the King very much. One day, Jonathan had gotten a message saying that Nicholas had a fatal disease and was enduring intense suffering. The sisters hoped that the Stranger could come and heal him like he had done so many other people. Or at the very least, they hoped the Stranger could give him the same comfort that they now had in the love of the King, and perhaps ease his passage to death. Jonathan begged the Stranger to go, but the Stranger seemed to be putting it off until Jonathan got another message in tear-stained ink, saying Nicholas had died.

Seemingly too late, the Stranger went to Arana and Kristi's house. Kristi had been stoic and silent, but Arana had thrown herself at the Stranger's feet. She had pleaded to know the reason he had not come when they asked. He had given a peculiar answer. "I have come, not to give glory to me, but to the King, who has the power over life and death."

This was where the facts differed. Some said he asked a friend to pose as the resurrected Nicholas. Others said the Stranger had gone to the tomb and called Nicholas back to life.

It was hard enough for people to acknowledge the fact that the Stranger *might* have been the King's Son, but to have the power to raise someone from the dead? Well, wasn't that too far-fetched?

"I'm done!" Contrand's booming voice echoed through the small shop and interrupted their thoughts. Jonathan and Aaren stood up, sighing in relief. Aaren looked outside, noting how low the sun had sunk in the mountains. "It's almost dusk. We have to hurry!"

Jonathan took the key from Contrand and handed it to Aaren. "Thanks again, Contrand. And by the way, remember the story of the King's mercy? Show some mercy on Titus, for he was the blind man the Stranger healed all those years ago, and you were the man who asked him how many fingers you were holding up to prove he could see!"

Contrand frowned. "For the Stranger's sake, I will show mercy and lessen his punishment, but it will still be something he will never forget!" Contrand's expression relaxed, and he suddenly laughed and slapped Jonathan on the back. "I'm sure if the Stranger could see how that stick of a man overpowered me, he would be chuckling. This is proof that my time with the Stranger changed me!"

"Or you just got fat and lazy," Jonathan said with a smirk, poking Contrand's stomach.

The Guide

Abi and Chris finally reached their destination. The mountains of Troche loomed over them like the craggy faces of menacing giants—intimidating and sinister.

"There better be some sort of path that leads to the castle," Abi said. "Because there is no way I'm climbing this mountain."

"For once, I agree with you. It's pretty steep and rocky. We don't have the skill to climb it. Let's look around."

As they walked, Abi suddenly said, "There's one thing I'm not sure about. How exactly did the Stranger die?"

"Didn't Micah say he died of a heart attack?"

"I doubt it. The lawmen had it in for him. Doesn't everything we've found out so far prove that?"

Chris mulled over that for a moment. "Yeah, I guess you're right. It would be awfully convenient for the lawmen if the Stranger died suddenly."

"See? The Stranger caused too much of a stir among the townspeople, and the lawmen feared they would revolt. So the lawmen decided to 'quietly do away with him' and blame it on a heart attack. But when the body disappeared, they blamed it on the Stranger's followers, who, of course, had nothing to do with it. Now the lawmen live in fear that someone knows how he died and will expose it."

A new voice interrupted their conversation. "That sounds like a suspenseful murder story."

Abi and Chris stopped mid-step, instinctively remembering the last time someone interrupted their conversation and what had happened afterward. Slowly they turned toward the voice, but Chris clutched his sister's hand, ready to run at the first sign of trouble.

A man calmly stepped out of the shadows of low-hanging branches, and his smile was reassuring and strangely familiar. He had shoulder-length dark hair and wore a robe with intertwining bright patterns—a contrast to the solid colors of the robes that the people in Meynch wore.

But what really took Abi aback were his eyes. Not so much the color, though. It was the fact that, even when she looked directly at them, she could not focus on them for more than a moment. Her vision just could not comprehend those eyes. They were ageless, fathomless, and filled with all strength and wisdom and love and joy and compassion in the universe. But they were veiled, as if the man was trying to hide his true nature. And although this should have made her suspicious, for some reason she could not bring herself to doubt a man with those eyes.

"Who are you?" she said, her tone almost reverent.

"Do not fear. I mean you no harm."

She looked at her brother. "*Should we trust him?*" she asked silently.

Chris bit his lip and stared at the man for a long moment. By Chris's pale face, Abi knew that Chris was encountering the same deep, poignant gaze Abi had seen.

He squeezed Abi's hand then said, "We believe you, sir. Though we don't know what you want with us." Chris tried to be respectful, for he knew without a doubt that this man was powerful and not one to be disrespected.

"I heard you talking about the Stranger, and I was interested in your opinion on him. He seemed like a rather…unique man."

"Well, we don't know much. He came here years ago and got the lawmen mad because he said he was the Son of the King. Everything we were saying was just theories."

"I may be able to help you, then. In the Book of the Law, it says…" He fished through his robe's pockets. "Now where did I put it?…Aha!" He pulled out a thick, leather-bound book, and the pages had yellowed with age.

"What Book of the Law?"

"The Book of the Law is a collection of the laws the King gave to the lawmen. Contained in this book are the Three Prophecies, given by the King himself, as well as smaller prophecies that confirm them by prophets and prophetesses over the centuries." The man carefully thumbed through the book. "One prophecy in particular became especially controversial when the Stranger came because he claimed it was about him.

Power abused, people mourn

With loss of innocence children born.

A cruel, dark power rears its head,

Its holy restraint almost dead.

He abandoned riches, a life of renown;

To bring hope, to give life,

The Son comes pure, but instead brings strife.

"According to the book, the Son sacrificed everything to come when Meynch was at its worst and bring hope. But a dark spirit would appear and stir up the people, so that they had to choose sides. The people would be divided in their loyalties."

"So are you saying the Stranger really *was* the Son of the King?" Chris asked.

"There are remarkable similarities, do you not agree?"

"Excuse me, sir, but then how did the Stranger…I mean, the Prince die?" Abi interrupted. "From what we've heard, the King and his Son ruled Meynch for centuries, which is more than any normal lifespan, so they must have been immortal or something."

"Yes, that is a mystery. I do not believe they are immortal. However, I do believe they have access to great power that most people do not. That power could be taken away…or willingly put aside."

"Are you saying the Prince gave up his crown *and* his power to come to Meynch?" Chris asked.

Abi looked at him and then her brother. "So did the lawmen kill him? I don't understand."

"Well," the older man said, "in theory, how would ruthless people quietly dispose of an unwanted threat?"

"In our world, they can use all kinds of things. There's poison, guns, strangling…" Abi covered her mouth quickly at the man's raised eyebrow. She had not meant to tell him that they were from another world. Had her slip of the tongue betrayed them?

But he said nothing about her accidental revelation. "Unfortunately, the lawmen have many of the same ways and even more creative ones. But they did not take into account the fact that, if the Stranger really was the King's Son, he could call upon his Father if ever he was in need. Ah, here we are!" The man pointed to a large castle that loomed over them.

"But…how…" Abi stopped and looked around. They had unknowingly climbed a steep path around the mountain as they had talked. She looked behind her but kept walking and almost ran into a large gate of pure, white stone.

"Whoa! Watch out, Abi!" Chris put out a hand to steady her as she fell back in shock. They stared at the gate. In addition to that, something was carved onto the gate—a murky picture that Abi could not make out. It was almost as if she were looking through someone's dirty glasses. Looking at Chris, she could tell he couldn't see the picture, either.

"Here." The man gave Chris a small pocketknife. "Cut me."

Chris's eyes widened, and his trembling fingers dropped the knife. "W-what!"

"Cut me. Not too deep, of course. I don't have a death wish. But enough to bleed." The man was strangely nonchalant, and it was unnerving.

Chris stared at him blankly. The man sighed and looked at Abi, who was equally perplexed by this turn of events. *His eyes* were *kind of freaky. Maybe he's insane. But would a crazy person be able to explain all that stuff about the Stranger so well? It makes no sense. He seemed so intelligent, but why would he ask us to make him bleed?*

"I know you probably are assuming the worst, and I realize this is a strange request, but it's the only way you can get in. Trust me, everything will be explained once you get inside."

Neither Chris nor Abi were convinced.

"I can say nothing else yet. You must trust me. There is much you need yet to know, and you do not have much time."

Chris inhaled through flared nostrils then slowly nodded. He bent down and picked up the knife. The man held out his hand.

"Where do you want me to cut?" Chris said with his hand shaking slightly.

"My palm."

Chris turned over the man's hand. What if he cut a vein and it wouldn't stop bleeding? The man would bleed to death!

"Trust me." The man's calm voice interrupted his morbid thoughts. Chris looked up and marveled at the man's serene, reassuring gaze. Against his better judgment, Chris felt strangely comforted.

He held the knife steady and ran the edge along the tender skin of the man's palm. A small rush of blood immediately began to flow out of the wound, and the man cupped his palm. "Good, that's enough. Abi, get the cup."

"What cup?" Abi was about to ask, and then she noticed a clear plastic cup that had been sitting on a tiny, barely noticeable platform by the gate. Without a word of protest, though all her questions seethed beneath the surface, she went, picked it up, and brought it back to Chris.

"Hold it steady. Don't let any spill," the man warned. He straightened his hand and let the blood flow into the cup. The blood filled the cup almost to the brim without one drop spilling to the floor.

"Now dip your fingers in it."

Chris gave Abi the knife but paled and looked up in horror when he heard the man's request. "What? Dip my fingers in it?"

He nodded.

"But—but—"

"Trust me." The man gazed at them both. "You have to trust me, or else your entire journey has been in vain."

Abi exploded. "Okay, listen, sir. With all due respect, we have been dragged here from our world, arrested, and thrown in jail, *twice*. We have found out that we don't even *belong* to our world, and then the very next day watched everyone who we had come to trust be arrested, too. *Then* we had to run for our *lives* and go into hiding! And you're saying that all that we've gone through is so we can stick our fingers in your blood?"

The man smiled. “Yes.”

Abi sputtered. “This is just crazy. Absolutely crazy! Just when I think I’ve seen everything!” She looked at her brother for backup.

Chris was unusually somber. “Why should we trust you?” he asked simply.

“Because only the King can help you now, and I will lead you to him.”

Chris sighed. He looked at the blood-filled cup like it was poison and then at the man, then back at the cup. Finally, he tentatively immersed his hand.

The man grinned from ear to ear as if they had passed some sort of test. “Smear it on the stone gate’s carving.”

Chris again obeyed, wiping the blood on the pure-white stone. All of a sudden, the image became clearer, and Abi gasped.

It was a lamb with a crown!

A loud clanking sound came from beyond the gate, and it steadily opened. When it was wide enough for three muscular men to walk in side-by-side, the man motioned them forward.

Abi reached out and held Chris’s shoulder when he was about to follow. “I still don’t know about this.”

“I know. But what choice do we have? He said everything would be explained once we got inside.”

“So I did, and so it will.” The man walked into the opening of the gate.

Chris hesitated, looked at Abi who was not moving yet, and followed the man through the gate and to the mysterious castle.

This is too much like the gate that brought us here, Abi thought. *But he said he can take us to the King, and the King's the only one who really knows what's going on in Meynch.* She sighed. *I hope we're making the right choice.*

Abi slowly stepped forward into the light.

Another Portal

The sun was low behind the mountains, painting the sky with vibrant hues of pink and violet when Nathan walked nonchalantly out of the courthouse. As soon as he closed the door, he began to run, looking behind him anxiously, and as a result ran right into Jonathan.

"I did it!" Nathan whispered.

"No one said anything?"

"I don't think so. But we have to hurry! I think Micah suspects something!"

"Okay, let's go!" Jonathan, Nathan, and Aaren dashed away from the courthouse.

A figure stood in the doorway of the courthouse, looking at the trio. He scowled. "They are not who they say they are."

A short, skinny servant ran up from behind the figure. "Micah, sir, I checked all our records of all the neighboring towns, even the ones beyond the mountains. There is no record of any royalty, and no one named Princess Vanna."

"Just as I thought. She, or he, had some insidious purpose in coming here." Micah thought for a moment. "They seemed to be rather interested in the prisoners. And since we know it was not really for a companion… Are all the prisoners still there?"

"Yes, sir."

"Do all the guards still have their keys?"

"Yes, sir."

A pause. Then, "What did they have with them?"

"They didn't have anything out of the ordinary, sir. The bodyguards had their swords, and the girl had a small handbag—"

"Fool!" Micah shouted, whirling to grab the trembling servant's shirt and lift him in the air with his eyes aflame. "What did she have in the handbag?"

"Uh…"

"You never thought to ask them, did you?"

"Well, I thought she had some ladies' things, you know…"

"Then tell one of the maids to ask her!" Micah expelled a loud, frustrated breath. "They could have slipped something to one of the prisoners. Lockpicks, daggers, anything could fit in a lady's purse!"

"Sir!" Another servant ran up. "The special prisoners have escaped!"

"*What*!" Micah exploded. "When did this happen?"

"We don't know, sir. The prisoners were secure when the guards checked them at high sun, but when they checked at dusk, they were gone."

"I knew it! That false princess slipped something to Kes and Marla! Check all the other prisons for any other empty cells. And you," Micah turned to the first servant. "Check that the girl is still secured comfortably."

"Yes, sir." Both servants hurried back into the courthouse.

Micah looked out on the town and saw in his mind's eye the old cottage Seginus claimed was his home. "Seginus, old man," Micah murmured. "You played a part in this. But I'm not finished yet. Your Stranger is dead and forgotten, and so is his so-called Father. Now it's our job to make sure they stay that way." Micah's lips curved into a evil smile as he retreated into the shadows of the courthouse doorway.

Jonathan stepped inside Seginus's cottage, followed by Aaren and Nathan. They immediately stepped on the square and dropped to the underground room.

Seginus was waiting for them and jumped up from the sofa he had been lounging on. "So? What happened?"

"We did it!" Nathan exclaimed.

"Let's not be too hasty. I want to hear everything that happened." Seginus turned to the men. "Jonathan? Aaren? Was Contrand there?"

"Titus had taken over his shop, but with a little prodding, he let Contrand go. We left Titus in the capable hands and justice of Contrand."

Seginus smiled. He also had been in the crowd that saw the blind beggar's healing, and he was not surprised Titus had turned to thievery. No lawman would accept any job application from him after that. He looked at Nathan intently. "Are you absolutely sure that you made a clean break, that the lawmen didn't have any inkling of what was really going on?"

"Actually..." Nathan hesitated. "Most of them fell for my disguise hook, line, and sinker, but I think Micah suspected something wasn't right. Micah asked me an odd question right before I left. He asked me, 'For a young lady, you have some very...masculine qualities.' I'm not sure if that meant he suspected something, or if he was trying to irritate me. I ignored him, of course."

Aaren cocked his head questioningly. "Maybe he suspects, but he does not know, or else he wouldn't ask. He knows Nathan is not a girl, but he doesn't know *who* he is. So we're safe."

"You don't understand," Seginus said. "Micah hates me. He knows everything about us because he pretended to be a stranger. He'll know I had something to do with this, and the first place he'll look is here." Seginus ran to one of the doors in the wall—the door no one had tried to hide in when Jonathan and the Stranger came. "You have to leave. Now. Behind this door is not a room but a portal to a place of safety. You must go through here, but be careful. You will see other portals to other places, but don't reach out or turn to them."

They looked at him blankly.

"Nathan, when you first met Abi and Chris, did they seem to appear out of the air?"

"Yeah!" Nathan's eyebrows scrunched together. "How did you know?"

"They came through a portal."

"What!"

"Listen very carefully. This underground chamber was not carved by human hands. The only thing I did to this place was add furniture and other necessities. The doors and the rooms behind the door were already here when I came thirty years ago. I found this portal when I decided to use the rooms as storage. One day I came to get something I had stored in the room only to find the room was empty. I was afraid to go inside for fear I'd disappear. So I sent in an thirteen-year-old orphan, whom I was the guardian of, warning him about the possible dangers. But he was willing. So I sent him through, and seconds later, he came out.

"'Why didn't you stay longer?' I asked him.

"'I stayed a whole day!' he replied.

"I was shocked. It had only been seconds here. So I had him write down everything he had seen while there. Sufficient to say, it was a magnificent tale. He had seen the King's castle and the King Himself! He said he had seen someone else, but he was told to seal his lips and heart until the time when that man would arrive in Meynch.

"When the Stranger came, the boy, who is now a young man, was quiet and somber. I asked him once if the Stranger was the man he had seen in the King's castle. He would not reply.

"He went to go see the Stranger one day and came back even more solemn then before. 'Sir,' he said to me, 'the Stranger is a ray of hope. But there is a darkness descending upon Meynch, and I cannot explain it. He will fight it, but I don't think he will fight it the way we expect. May the King protect us all.'

"Two days later, the lawmen had a secret trial of some sort. As a result of this, Micah himself killed John, the boy I had sent through the portal. Do you know why? Because he claimed to have seen the King and lived.

"Micah found out I was the one who supposedly sent him to see the King, and he brought me on trial. I could honestly say all I did was send the boy into a room, and he came out, claiming to have seen the King. The lawmen all said I was innocent, except Micah. He knew I was keeping something from him. But they didn't believe him, and I was released.

"Ever since then, Micah has hated me. He slowly lost his standing in the lawmen's courts. But soon after the Stranger came, he said he had turned a new leaf. He pretended to be the same man I had befriended long ago and professed his belief in the Stranger's teachings. Now of course, we know better. I should not have allowed myself to be so easily deceived, but I wanted to believe the best of him, despite his animosity towards me."

Nathan and Aaren gawked at Seginus's story.

"But I have wasted enough time reminiscing. You need to hurry." Seginus threw open the door.

The room was filled with cobwebs, the inside looked decayed, and the paint was peeling. Nathan looked at Seginus questioningly. "Just one last question. Why didn't you just send Abi and Chris through here, so they could go straight to the King's castle?"

Seginus smiled. "They needed to meet someone important in their journey. Now, remember, don't trust appearances. Not everything is as it seems."

Jonathan walked backward a few feet then ran straight into the room and disappeared. Aaren followed, jogging into the room with not as much momentum. Nathan looked at Seginus then at the room. *I wonder if every door has a portal behind it,* he wondered as he entered the room.

That was his last thought in Seginus's house.

Just as Nathan disappeared, Seginus heard a knock at his door. He had made a way for him to hear anyone knocking in the underground chamber using a sound tunnel. He smiled. *Just in time. They'll know not to come back.*

Seginus stepped into the square and milliseconds later was above ground. He opened the door. At the sight of the middle-aged couple, he sighed in relief.

"Kes! Marla! I thought you were…I'm expecting visitors of a nasty sort. Anyway, don't come in yet. Just listen for a second. Once you come in, you will drop to my underground chamber. You will see three doors in the wall in front of you. Go into the middle one. It is a portal to a place of safety." Kes looked at Seginus questioningly. "No time to explain. Hurry!"

Kes nodded and took Marla's hand. Seginus moved aside, and they stepped in the square and disappeared.

Seginus waited, his heart racing, by the door. He had a plan, one that was foolhardy and brash, but he was prepared to make it work. Minutes later, someone banged loudly on the door.

"I'm coming, I'm coming." Seginus opened the door slightly.

"Hello, Micah. What a surprise."

The pale-skinned, muscular man pushed open the door completely and stared at Seginus with ice-blue eyes that were filled with hate. "Where are they?"

"Who?" Seginus asked innocently. "Oh, forgive my manners. Come in, come in." While Seginus greeted Micah, he turned the square with his foot. *This'll take us right in front of the doors.*

Micah stepped into the house and a fraction of a moment later was in Seginus's underground chamber.

"I see your standards have lowered since I last visited your home. This place is a mess."

"Like the Stranger taught, a dirty house filled with good people is better than an expensively decorated house in which liars live."

Micah looked at Seginus in a new light. "Well, you've finally realized what was right in front of you."

"That the traitor in our midst was my former friend?" Seginus clenched his jaw. "Yes, I have. I wanted too much to restore the friendship with the man who I trusted more than any other."

Micah half-smiled. "See, that is where you stumbled. I am not that man any longer. Your naivety and eagerness to see the best in others, something your beloved Stranger also shared with you, led to your downfall. The only reason I waited until now was that I wanted to relish your demise, and I could not fully enjoy it if you were still unaware. But do not think you have distracted me. Where are the fake princess and Jonathan and Aaren, old man?"

"I don't know any princesses."

"I know you don't. But you know a *fake* one. Now, once again, I ask you, *where are they*?"

Seginus was slowly backing up as he talked to Micah. He knew the door was only a few feet behind him. He had a plan, which was a long shot to be sure, but it might work.

"I—oh!" Seginus pretended to trip and fell back against the door. As he thought, the door was not strong enough to withstand his weight and opened. He stepped backward and closed the door in Micah's face before being sucked into the portal. He heard, more than saw, Micah open the door and enter the portal, as well.

The King's Revelation

Abi, Chris, and their mysterious guide entered the castle courtyard. Chris, who was usually the more articulate of the two, could only say what Abi was thinking. "Wow!"

Oak trees stood guard beside the castle entrance, and to their left there was a white stone bench with a pillow backing. Brightly colored flowers flourished around a large fountain that looked like a waterfall to their right. Everything beyond that simply defied description. It seemed to be the best of nature wrapped up in a small space. No, it was more than that; it was the very heart of nature—glowing, pure, and full of life. *This is what the Garden of Eden must have looked like,* Abi thought.

The Man led them to the castle entrance and opened the golden doors.

The portal propeled Nathan, Jonathan, and Aaren along at breath-taking speed. It was like a slide, except there was no clear bottom, and if they had stopped moving at any moment, Nathan was afraid they would drop down into the bottomless dark abyss beneath them. He clenched his pants tightly and tried not to think about how they balanced on nothing but air.

All around them, bright rays of white and purple light shot forward, sparkling and fizzing like firecrackers. They saw Kes and his wife, and Jonathan tried to call to them, but the words caught in his throat.

Kes looked around as he was pushed forward against his will through the portal. He saw Nathan with Jonathan and Aaren a few feet away from him and turned to Marla. His wife, fear written all over her face, was looking beneath them at the bottomless abyss and shuddering violently. He wrapped an arm around her and tried to whisper reassuring words, but he couldn't move his mouth to speak.

Seginus's head jerked backward as he was thrust through the portal. He knew better than to look down, so instead he looked ahead. He saw Nathan, Jonathan, Aaren, Kes, and Marla in front of him and turned to see Micah behind him. But he knew not to try to speak to them, as Jonathan's brother had mentioned the lack of sound in the portal. *I hope the King will deal with Micah.*

What magic is this? Micah thought as he was propelled through the portal. He saw the abyss beneath him and took a deep breath, pushing down his fear. *Fear is weak-*

ness, and weakness I cannot afford right now. How did I get in here? Swatting aside the pesky bolts of light, he saw Seginus ahead of him. *What sorcery did you do, old man?*

Abi thought the courtyard was impressive, but when compared to the castle's interior, the courtyard was nothing.

It was a magnificent chamber and was elaborately decorated with fine Persian rugs and scarlet tapestries with intricate designs. The white, stone walls were lined with a wavy amber-colored border. A beautiful mural of a crimson and violet sunset surrounded a golden throne on a high dais, glowing with pure white light, which was almost blinding in its intensity. Abi and Chris threw up their arms to cover their eyes from the brilliant radiance.

After a long moment, the light dimmed. "Welcome, travelers." The voice was as loud as a thundering waterfall, but yet as soft as a mother's caress, deep and powerful, yet kind and gentle. It was the voice they had heard while in Seginus's house surrounded by shadows.

Abi looked up to see a man sitting on the throne. He wore a large, jeweled crown and richly colored robes, which were brighter even than their guide's. His face was ageless, being both old and young and yet neither. And his eyes were almost exactly the same as their guide's except a thousand times more unbearable because they were not veiled.

Abi knew that she stood in the presence of the King—the very essence of goodness, of holiness. *And who knew purity could be so painful?* She felt his gaze pierce to her heart as he effortlessly viewed her deepest thoughts and secrets and revealed them to her as well. It was not an easy or pretty sight. Ugly things that Abi had pushed deep within her heart were now brought to the forefront. Yet the King's eyes held no condemnation; in fact, they were overflowing with love and compassion.

Abi could not bear to look at those eyes any longer. She looked at their guide and suddenly made the connection. Their eyes, their robes, their power…"You're the Prince, the King's son," she said, looking at their guide. "You're the Stranger."

Chris turned to look at him as well with awe and not a little fear, but no surprise. *The King's Son!*

The Prince bowed to his Father and smiled at them. He walked to the dais to stand beside and just below the King.

The King looked at them and smiled. "Christopher Candial. Abigale Candial. You have journeyed far, and I can imagine you have many questions."

Abi stood, gaping at the King and the Son, but out of the corner of her eye she saw Chris bow low. She closed her mouth, blinked, and curtsied deeply. Somehow she did not mind when the King said her full name. "Yes, your highness. I mean, I have a lot of questions. With all due respect—"

"Wait." The King held up a hand and looked beyond them. Abi followed the King's gaze to the wall behind them. "They have breached the portal."

What? Abi and Chris looked at each other then back at the seemingly ordinary white wall.

Suddenly a white glowing swirl appeared, and a group of people appeared behind it, seemingly far in the distance. Abi recognized Nathan, Jonathan, and Aaren, and as they appeared to come closer, she saw Kes and Marla, Seginus, and…

"Micah?"

❧ ❧ ❧ ❧

Nathan popped out of the portal first and then Jonathan and Aaren. When they saw the King and the Prince, their eyes widened, but Jonathan bowed, and Aaren and Nathan followed suit. Nathan ran to Abi and Chris. "What's going on?" he asked them.

"We don't know," Chris replied, and Abi just shrugged.

Kes and Marla jumped out of the portal. Kes bowed, and Marla curtsied to the King and the Son. Soon after came Seginus, who did not look at all surprised to see the royal family. He bowed deeply and smiled at the Prince. "Your majesties. I am your humble servant."

Suddenly, a loud rumble shook the portal, and Seginus, Kes, and Marla ran to join the teens at the foot of the King's dais. They all watched the portal, knowing and dreading the next arrival.

A tall, muscular, pale-skinned man stepped out of the portal, his clenched fists showing his malice even before they saw his ice blue eyes rimmed in black.

"You!" Micah shouted at the Son. "We killed you!"

Abi gasped.

"Death has no power here. My Father has the power over life and death."

"Blasphemy! No one has the power of life and death!"

"No one but me," the King replied.

If Abi had not been looking at Micah closely, she might have missed what happened at the King's words. Micah's eyes darkened from ice blue to black onyx, and he began to glow with an eerie violet light tinged in black.

"You are nothing, old man. The people have forgotten you, reveling now in their lust for power as we recruit more of them to us. No one remembers You. Your precious son did nothing but remind them of what they abandoned, and after we killed Him, they soon turned back to us to drown out their guilty consciences."

The King sighed. "Yet I love them, and I brought these two children from their world to this one to bring them back to me."

"Yes, but for what? No one cares. The people resist You. They hate You. Give up."

The King stood, righteous anger filling his face. "Enough. Reveal your true nature, spirit, and silence your lies!"

"Oh, a challenge. I shall take you up on that, oh King." Micah's eerie glow grew larger and more substantial. Micah collapsed on the ground, convulsing and twitching, and his face contorted in obvious pain while the eerie glow transformed into a shadowy, vaguely outlined dark spirit with burning, violet eyes.

The being's voice deepened until it reverberated through the chamber. "Ah, I have returned. Do you dare challenge me yourself, oh King, or will you send your weakling son or his followers to do it again? I have crushed them all before, and I will do it again."

The King looked at the being sadly, and his visage was a mix of anger and sorrow. "Do not test me, spirit. Though I know the depths of your irredeemable wickedness, those here do not."

"Why don't you tell them then? Why don't you tell them how I single handedly changed the face of this world and turned Meynch against you? Why don't you tell them of my unmatched power?"

The King actually chuckled, albeit sadly. "Your pride embellishes what truly happened. For you know as well as I that once you were nothing but an ordinary human. You were called Reuben on Earth. You met Scott Candial, Abi and Chris's father, when he first came to your world as a young man, and you became friends.

"You have always had a perverted streak in you. You tried every twisted thing that the world had to offer: drugs, alcohol, sex in all its tainted forms, and you were addicted to all of them. Scott saw this and tried to warn you, but you would not listen. Your life was spiraling downhill, yet you refused to see your problems. As a result, he broke off your friendship.

"You could not let go of Scott that easily, though. You became an odd sort of stalker, clinging to the one miniscule shred of decency by keeping track of his life. You saw his happiness when he married, and his financial success, and you were jealous.

"One day you saw Scott and his wife disappear in a flash of light as they stood on a portal, which you thought was an old gravestone. You were at first interested about what he had stumbled upon, and then obsessed. But for many years, you were too drunk or high to think, much less investigate a portal. Finally, curiosity won out, and you became sober for the sole purpose of finding out where Scott had gone.

"Looking back, don't you realize how easy it was for them to take away your soul? You had but a small ember of goodness in you, but it was something. You even came here for help. But the spirits had found a foothold and latched on—your anger at Scott Candial for supposedly abandoning you. You didn't understand that if he had allowed his friendship to flourish, you would have both drowned in your miserable life. But he did the right thing, and instead of acknowledging your sin and repenting, you accused him of all manner of self-serving things.

"So in return for revenge, you surrendered to the seductive whispers of the spirits, and they made you a ghost just like them. They changed your name to Reilim and changed your very identity. You have no life, no essence. You are now nothing but a soulless puppet."

"A puppet I may be, in your eyes, but my masters have given me power over the masses and made me the ruler of the darkness of this world! All you offered was a lonely, bland life of good deeds and 'spreading kindness throughout the world.' Pathetic."

The King continued as if he had not interrupted. "You found the perfect opportunity to have vengeance soon after you inhabited the body of Micah and formed a close friendship with Scott. But this time you determined you would break Scott's heart, not the other way around, biding your time patiently.

"And you succeeded. You broke off Scott's friendship, drove him out of Meynch, and corrupted the lawmen. You caused so much damage to my kingdom in such a short period of time.

"After he left, you relaxed, sometimes controlling Micah and other times Judge Faln or even other lawmen. You were fueled by the evil within you, now being without hope of salvation, and so you determined to make the people as miserable as you, ruling with an iron fist.

"Then my son came. You snapped into action, but too late. He had already reminded the people of what they had been before you came and how close they had been with me. He told them once more of my love and compassion for them, even then, when they were knee-deep in sin and despair. You could do nothing to erase the hope he had left on the people's hearts, but you could eliminate him from giving more. So you killed him, not realizing that the same day you killed my son, another Son in another world was celebrating the day He died and was brought back to life by the power of His Father's love.

"You were shocked and infuriated when you saw my son was alive, and you set your sights on the prophecy I gave the people so long ago and anticipated the arrival of Abi and Chris. This time you determined to be ready for them and stirred up the people against their coming.

"You have tried everything, yet you still will ultimately lose, for when you gave up your soul, you gave up any hope of going back to your world and recovering from the awful mess you had made of your life. Now you have no life and are doomed forever to wander, cursing your Maker and longing for a redemption that you will never have."

The being smirked. "Thank you for your boring monologue, but you are wrong. I do not long for my former life. I despise it! Then I was weak, but now I have power beyond anything any of you can imagine with an army of indestructible spirits at my command. There is nothing I cannot control—nothing I cannot have—"

Chris rolled his eyes. "Um, not to state the obvious, but you kind of sold your soul. Big downside. World domination is totally not worth it."

"Chris," Abi hissed, "this is not a joke."

Chris nodded, and his face grew somber. "We don't want what you are offering, Reilim. We were summoned here to reveal the secret you have kept so long from the people—the secret of the Stranger's death. No matter what happens, if you kill us or whatever, we stand with the King and His Son. Heck, we aren't even from this world. Why would we want to control it? We just want to go home. But, if anyone remembers us here, we'd like to be remembered because we were faithful to the King and the Stranger to the end, not because we were traitors like you."

Seginus smiled. He knew that he and his friends were here simply as witnesses, and he was proud to see the courage of the children.

Reilim sighed sadly. "I'm hurt that you don't trust me. Yet I see the truth of things. Chris, you have rejected me. Very well. But you cannot speak for your sister. Like Eve in the garden, Abi, you must decide for yourself."

The spirit's voice became smooth, cajoling. Shadows clouded Abi's mind as, almost without her realizing it, she began to listen to the persuasive voice.

"Yes, Abi. To you I will give what you have always desired. You escape to your imagination because there you can be whoever you wish. You want to fit in and be like everyone else. I can give you this. You want to go home. I can do that, as well. Do you really think the King will send you home? He wants you to fulfill his prophecy. He will never let you return. But not only will I send you back, I will also give you the means to become the most powerful young woman Earth has ever known. Astonishing beauty. Matchless intelligence. The charisma that will send you skyrocketing up the social ladder. Isn't that what every girl wants?"

"Abi, you're not really listening to this, are you?" Chris looked at his sister who had a strange gleam in her eyes. "Abi? Come on, you don't need all that junk."

"What every girl wants..." she murmured.

Reilim smiled. He had found a foothold. *It's almost too easy*, he thought. *Like Eve in the garden.*

"No! Abi, snap out of it! He's trying to trick you!"

"But…" Abi's green eyes were glazed with a violet sheen.

Chris was becoming frantic. "Someone do something!"

Kes tried to step forward, but he could not move. Neither could his wife or Seginus and his friends. He looked to the King beseechingly. "She needs us!"

The King's eyes were filled with pain, but he said, "This must be her decision. I will reach out to her with all that I am, but I cannot change what is in her heart."

"What!" Chris shouted. "You're kidding me! We did *not* come all this way for this! What kind of King are you?" He shook Abi's shoulders. "Wake up! Don't listen to him!"

Abi's gaze was fastened to Reilim, and she broke Chris's hold and took a step toward him. Then another. Chris saw that she looked exactly the same as she did when she was having a vision, except he knew this was a vision of the darkest kind…

Someone was calling Abi's name, but she could not hear them. She was focused on the glowing mirror in front of her. A girl stared back at her—a girl with stunning cheekbones, perfect hair, a body with curves in all the right places, and Abi's wide, hazel eyes.

"This is who you want to be: beautiful, accomplished, captivating. This is who I can make you."

I know he's evil and wrong, but... Abi remembered all the times she had seen the pretty girls, the ones who charmed everyone with their beatuy and tinkling laughs as they simply walked through the halls. She remembered her own insecurity in the face of those popular girls. But most of all, she remembered all the times anyone ever made fun of her for being the weirdo who zoned out in the middle of class, the girl who lived in la-la land.

With this, I could be popular. Envied. Untouchable. The charmer instead of the charmed.

But at what cost?

What does it matter? a dark, sensous voice replied. *This is what you've always wanted. Take it while you still can!*

The mirror shrank until it was no bigger than her fist and floated only a few feet away.

"Take the mirror. Take the power I offer you."

Pushing aside her reservations, Abi reached out and snatched the object out of the air. Violet light flashed, blinding her.

Abi was in her bedroom. *What?* Abi blinked. *How did I get here? I'm not dreaming, am I?* She pinched herself. "Ow! I guess not."

Walking over to the mirror above her dresser, she stared disbelieving at her reflection. It was the gorgeous girl Reilim had showed her!

He did it! He brought me back! He kept his promise!

That's more than the King ever did. Maybe I had it wrong the whole time. Maybe the King isn't all he was made out to be.

Abi stepped out her bedroom and looked around. *Wait a second, where is everyone?*

She hurried down the stairs and into the kitchen. She found her dad sitting at the table, his head in his hands. Chris was patting his back awkwardly. Chris looked older, buffer, and he wore a formal tie and suit. Scott Candial's hair was streaked with gray, and his face was haggard.

She went to him and touched his shoulder. "Dad? What's wrong?" she asked.

He did not respond.

"Hello? Dad?" She shook his shoulder. "It's me, Abi."

It was as if she was not even there. *The only time people can't see or hear me is in my visions. But this is real… isn't it?*

"It's not your fault, Dad," Chris said. "It was Abi's choice."

Abi realized her father was crying. "I just don't understand. She may have daydreamed a little too often, but she was never a rebellious child. Her heart was good. I never thought she would do something like this." His voice broke.

"Ever since that Saturday morning in the backyard, she's been acting differently," Chris said softly. "I don't remember exactly what happened, and she won't tell me, but something *did* happen. I just wish I could remember…"

What? So neither Chris nor Dad remember going to Meynch? What did I do that was so bad? What's going on?

Abi threw her arm to cover her face as violet light flashed, blinding her.

She was back in the world of murky shadows and the glowing mirror. But now her face looked the same, and the mirror was glowing with a soft, golden hue instead of violet.

"What's going on?" she cried. "I don't understand!"

A voice as loud as thunder and as soft as a caress spoke to her. "Child, that is only a small taste of what will come if you accept Reilim's power."

The difference between this comforting voice and the evil hiss was so obvious now. "I don't understand, your Majesty. What happened? Was this a vision of the future? What did I do that was so bad?"

Slowly a figure appeared before her—a man in a crown and royal robes with warm brown eyes filled with all the love of the ages. "The future I showed is not certain, and it takes place several years from now. The details are not for you to know. Suffice it to say, child, by agreeing to Reilim's offer, you would allow yourself to be possessed by a spirit that no mortal should ever have within them. Your mind and soul would be sacrificed on the altar of selfish lusts, much like Reilim himself. Your father was suffering because he saw you discard the love of those precious to you and destroy your own life in the process."

Abi bit her lip. "Wait, I didn't want that. I never wanted to be possessed. I just wanted to be normal, to be popular. I mean, is it so wrong to want that?"

"Abigale." The King smiled tenderly. "You were never normal. Your extraordinary imagination is the very reason I brought you here. For only those who are willing to believe the unbelievable can truly see me. Normal is shallow, bland, and empty. All those people you envy so much, they have no potential in my eyes because they can only see temporary pleasure. The next boyfriend, the next party, the next shopping spree, the list goes on and on.

"But you? You look beyond that. You are creative and inspiring, although you may not exactly choose the right times to unleash your whimsy."

Abi bit her lip. "Yeah…sorry about that."

"The reason I chose you is because I wanted to give you the chance to live your dreams, to test your limits beyond your day-to-day routine. I chose you for a life of adventure, of learning to love and be loved, to enjoy life abundantly.

"Your life will be different now that you have come to Meynch. This is your first step onto a path that will take you somewhere you never imagined you will be. And yes, this path is harder than the other. This path requires sacrifice and maturity, seeds of which have been planted in both you and your brother. You will be called to do things you will not want to do. But out of these things will come great joy. You have been chosen for greater things to come."

"I have been chosen," Abi murmured to herself. "I have been chosen for greater things. The King chose me. He brought me here for a reason. I have been chosen."

The King stretched out his hand. Abi was startled to see blood oozing from a fresh, ragged wound in his palm. "Take my hand, Abi. Embrace the truth and flee from evil."

Abi hesitated. "How do I know you are telling the truth?"

"My word is truth. My blood is my bond. I cannot break my promises, and I will never forsake those who trust in me."

She searched his eyes.

"He won't give you what you want!" a voice hissed behind her.

"No." Abi firmed her resolve. "I wanted fantasy; he offers reality. What I wanted is nothing compared to the adventure that lies before me. I'm done dreaming about adventure...I want to live it."

Abi reached out and touched his fingertips.

The darkness exploded in a flash of light.

Abi's eyes flew open. She was lying on a cold floor, and a male face loomed above her that was filled with concern and pain. "Ch—Chris?"

"Abi!" Chris helped her sit up. "Are you all right?"

"Yeah. I think I'm fine." Abi rubbed her forehead. "What happened?"

Abi gasped as her memory came rushing back. She leaped to her feet and glared at Reilim. "You!"

The King raised a hand, and she paused. His eyes blazed with righteous anger, but it was directed toward the demonic spirit. "Reilim, for your desecration of my laws, for the evil you planted in my people, I banish you forever to the abyss beyond the edge of our land, in the Great Sea of Darkness. There you will be bound for a hundred years until you are released once more for the final battle." The King clenched his fist.

Reilim screamed in agonized defiance. Long rope-like beams of blazing white light wove around his phantom essence, binding him. Tighter and tighter they wrapped around him, until from inside the being came an explosion of blinding violet light and suffocating gray fog.

When Abi's vision cleared, all that was left was a wisp of dark smoke that moved to curl around Micah who huddled in a corner of the chamber.

The King turned his piercing gaze to Micah. "As for you..."

Micah threw himself on his face before the dais. "Your Majesty, I beg for mercy. All the evil I have done was under the spirit's control. Now that I am free of him, I will serve you faithfully for all of my days."

"Pitiful," Chris mumbled.

The King shook his head slowly. "The only way Reilim could inhabit you was if you had already bargained your soul away to the spirits. You are far from blameless in the evil that has been unleashed. Yet death will not be your fate, though you may wish for it. You are cursed to forever wear the mark of the spirits you served on your forehead and wander the mountains of Troche until the day when you choose whom you will serve."

Micah was pushed by an unseen hand against the wall with his arms spread out, and on his forehead appeared a fiery mark that was shaped like a jagged circle. He cried out in pain and disappeared.

The King sighed and spoke softly. "I have wonderful plans for every person in Meynch. But even while I craft these plans and guide them to fulfill them, I know. I reach out to them with everything that I have, yet I know. I know who will push my hand away, and the pain they suffer because of their choice pains me as well because I know what they could have been."

He turned back to the crowd of people who were gaping at the other side of the chamber. "Abigale, Chris."

Abi and Chris approached the golden throne of the King. Abi was still a little fearful, but the kindness coming from the King's eyes reassured her. He smiled.

"There is much you have seen that you do not understand, correct?"

They nodded.

"Don't be afraid. Ask." The King motioned for them to come forward. The Stranger, who had been watching from behind the throne, moved to sit at the King's right-hand where there suddenly appeared another throne that was equal in size.

Abi cleared her throat, then spoke. "Umm…thank you, your Majesty, for saving me from Reilim. I'm sorry I doubted you. But yeah, I do have a couple questions. I mean, besides the obvious question of why we are in another world, which has already been answered by my dad when he told us that we were born here. I don't understand how both you and Reilim got your power. Is it magic? And who are the spirits? I had a vision that kind of said something about them, that they were the real enemies of Meynch, and then Reilim came. He's obviously a evil spirit. But I don't really understand how the magic here works."

"That is a concept even the wisest of this land struggle to understand. The magic that you are thinking of, with wands and broomsticks and the like, does not exist here. However, Meynch is made of two worlds intertwined: the physical world you can see and the spiritual world you cannot. When the land is governed by honorable people who employ both justice and mercy in their dealings with the people, this goodness manifests itself in the spiritual world as benevolent beings that guide the people of Meynch. In the same way, evil has flourished for too long, fueling on the malice of the lawmen, and so beings of unimaginable wickedness and power have emerged. One of those is Reilim.

"The complex part is that both the physical and the spiritual are so interwined that a physical being has some of the spiritual in them. It is, sadly, very easy to abandon one's humanity and become a completely spiritual being. Although he began as a human, anyone who willingly gives their soul to evil through rituals of blood becomes a spirit of darkness."

"A ritual of blood?"

The Stranger spoke up. "Blood is the seal of the spirit world. That is why you had to smear my blood on the gate to reveal the crest. Only my blood keeps Meynch from being overcome."

"So you *did* die," Chris said wonderingly.

The Stranger smiled. "My father alone has the power over life and death."

Chris's eyebrows scrunched up—a sure sign he was confused.

"For now, it will suffice to say that I and my son have power in both the spiritual and physical worlds," the King said. "The rest will be revealed to you in time."

"I have a feeling he's not going to tell us any more than that," Chris muttered. "So, sir," he turned back to the King, "we've seen the spirits of darkness. But where are the good ones?"

"Spirits are at work around us even as we speak. Look."

Suddenly the blazing white glow surrounding the throne intensified, and Abi, squinting against the light, saw the outline of four figures in golden tunics and white cloaks edged in gold. She looked beside her and was startled to see two figures, like guards, beside her. She glanced at Chris and distinguished two spirit guards beside him, as well.

As suddenly as it had come, the mist disappeared, and with it the spirit guards, leaving everyone breathless with wonder.

Abi tapped her chin with her index finger and suddenly blurted out, "Sir, why have I been having visions? I don't get it. I like to daydream, but I've seen you and the Stranger, I mean, the Prince, Meynch, and the Three Prophecies in my dreams, and it's really weird because I don't know what they're for."

The King smiled sympathetically but shook his head. "That I cannot explain. Not yet, at least. Your work in this world is not done, and you will see much more in the next few years here in Meynch and in your world. But pay very close attention to your dreams, for no longer will you dream of irrelevant things."

"You can't tell me or won't?" Abi asked. Realizing how disrespectful that sounded, she added, "Not meaning to be rude, sir."

The King stared intently at her. His eyes were deep-brown, gentle, and kind, yet firm. She was frightened by all the power and emotion reflected there, yet it was the fear of awe and worship, and she had to fight the urge to throw herself prostrate on the ground before him.

Abi averted her eyes.

"My child. You have taken your first steps on this new path, yet I see the shadows of doubt still in your heart. You must ask, or else you give a foothold to evil, and you will certainly fall."

Abi shrugged, still not looking at Him. "We did what we came to do, but I'm still confused. What do we do from here? Do we stay in Meynch? Is this our home? Or do we go back to our own world? Oh, and what about Weana? Is she all right?"

"Do not worry. You will return to your own world. But as I have told you, you have been chosen, and you can never go back to how things were before. Your adventure has just begun. As for Weana, her time will come. She still has a great part to play very soon. But you still have time to think about it. Your initial task, the reason you were first brought to this world, is not yet complete. There is yet one more thing you all must do." The King motioned them all closer.

They sat at the top step of the King's dais, at his feet. "Now," the King began, "this is what you will do…"

The Confrontation

A young boy ran through the streets, murmuring a hurried, "Pardon me," after colliding into people several times, but he could not pause to apologize further. His mission was too important.

He had to find the lawmen and tell them of the disturbance in the town. The people were rising up, being led by someone unimaginable. He ran faster, bursting into the courthouse. The darkly handsome Judge Faln sat at the head of the rest of the lawmen as they dicussed the affairs of Meynch.

"Sirs?" the boy said loudly.

All heads turned to face him. The lawmen looked up from their meeting, scowling when they saw the source of the interruption. "What do you want?" Faln barked.

"The stranger kids are here, and they want to see you. They have something to tell you and all the people, and everybody's rushing to get here because they said … they said … they…" The boy stopped at the lawmen's murderous looks.

Judge Faln stood and motioned for one of the servants serving them tea to give the boy a gold coin. The boy took it with a big grin on his face and bowed to the lawmen. "Sirs." Then he rushed out of the chamber.

"So the children are coming. They have escaped the sentinels I had posted along the main road and are coming to wreak havoc on Meynch just like the Stranger," Judge Faln said placidly.

"We should have killed them while we had the chance," another lawmen commented angrily, banging his clenched fists on the table.

"No. If we had, we would not have found out the valuable information we have." Faln gestured to the servant, and he came quickly and bowed low. "Master."

"Go and bring the special prisoners immediately."

"But master, the special prisoners have escaped."

Faln's eyes burned with sudden fury. "And why wasn't I notified of this? It had better be a good reason, or it'll be your head."

"Master, we told Micah, and we assumed—"

Faln looked out over the assembly and noticed one seat was empty."And where is Micah today?"

"He went to find out what had happened to them."

"Are you positive *all* the special prisoners escaped?"

"Yes, master. The girl and her parents are gone."

Faln banged his fist on the table in rage. "Curse you, incompetent fools! Now we have no idea what those brats are planning!"

Suddenly the doors flew open again, and a young girl stood in the doorway beside a taller, lean boy. "We're here to reveal your secrets," Abi said confidently.

Faln feebly sank into his chair like a much older man, but there was a wicked gleam in his eyes that said that the battle was far from over.

The courthouse was packed to its limit. Seconds after Abi and Chris's dramatic entrance, crowds of people from all reaches of Meynch had poured into the courthouse to see the stranger children who claimed to fulfill one of the prophecies.

Chris, as the oldest child and only male of the two siblings, would have to lead the prosecution. Abi was amazed at the change that was becoming evident in her brother. She saw very little of the immature boy he had been before they had come to Meynch, and in his place was a determined, reliable young man who was willing to take on whatever responsibility was handed to him. The success of their endeavor rested on Chris following the King's instructions to the last letter, and Abi had no doubt left in her mind that Chris could do it.

Abi observed the professional-looking courthouse. There was a judge's bench on a high platform, behind which an old man in white robes sat. To its right was something resembling a jury box, inside which a group of people also in white robes sat. Below the platform were three pulpits. Chris sat behind the one on the far left, but the middle and far right pulpits were empty.

Abi looked closely at the judge. It was not Faln, she knew, for he was sitting in the crowd. But who was it?

The judge unexpectedly turned his head to meet her gaze and winked.

Chris stood up after the chamber had quieted and announced boldly, "On behalf of the King and His Son, whom you called the Stranger, we have come to bring before the court the lawmen. They have been charged with abusing the power entrusted to them by the King and twisting the laws to fit their own purposes."

The shock of his accusation reverberated through the chamber. This child actually dared to stand up to the lawmen! No one spoke for several minutes.

Quickly Faln stood up. "I object!" he shouted angrily. "I object most strongly!"

Chris acknowledged him, saying, "According to the law, to combat this man's objection, at least seven men in this room must publicly agree with my accusation and state their cause. If none do, I will stand back and subject myself to the lawmen."

"How does he know this much about the law? He's only been here a few days," Faln whispered angrily to a lawman next to him.

A man stood up from the crowd. "I agree with this ma—er, boy's accusation." Abi, sitting right behind Chris, attempted to discern who he was. But he soon answered it for her. "My name is Titus, and I agree because I was unfairly and roughly treated for truthfully claiming that I had been healed from my blindness by the Stranger, which is against the law unless I had a trial, which I—"

"Did!" Faln interjected loudly.

The Judge glared at him. "You may not speak."

Faln quieted and sulked like a little boy.

Another man stood up, as well. "I agree with this boy's accusation. My name is Contrand, and I agree because my business was almost taken away by the lawmen because they found out I believed the Stranger was the King's Son."

"Judge," Faln interrupted, spitting out the word, "all these men's agreements center around issues relating to the Stranger. I admit we acted uncharacteristically while He was here. We were desperate to uproot the troublemaker. Therefore, I please request that all further agreements be about any other instances of mistreatment outside the period of time when the Stranger was here." The rest of his request was in a syrupy smooth voice.

The Judge thought for a moment then shook his head. "All witnesses are valid as long as their cause is factual and accurate. However, it would be better for the prosecution if they had witnesses with causes that took place before or after the Stranger's arrival and death."

Abi saw Faln wanted to argue his point, but she knew he would not. Faln knew that the Judge had come up with a fair compromise, and he could not argue at the risk of losing face among the jury and his fellow lawmen. She smiled. Their trap was ready.

She paid little to no attention to the next five witnesses, but she did notice none of them mentioned incidents during the Stranger's time in Meynch. If anything, the incidents before the Stranger came were worse than any during the Stranger's stay.

"Since my accusation has been backed by seven upstanding members of the community, I now have the right to call forth my witnesses, whom the defense may lawfully question. However, the law states that if any questioning goes to personal matters unrelated to the issue at hand, I have the right to withdraw the witness from any further questioning, and the witness will still be considered valid."

Chris glanced at Faln as he spoke the last sentence. They both knew what he meant, and Faln's eyes narrowed. The lawmen would not be allowed to question Abi and Chris's witnesses about their relationship to the Stranger.

"I call forth my first witness. Seginus Davidson. This man has been an upstanding member of Meynch for many years and was a lawmen himself for seventeen years until a controversial issue forced him to resign. Even then, many people have gone to him for legal and personal advice, and he has been known for his wisdom and fairness."

One of the doors behind the jury box opened and out stepped Seginus, who went to stand behind the middle pulpit.

Chris sat down tiredly and wiped his forehead, his work done for now. Abi reached over and clasped his hand. He looked at her, and she smiled reassuringly. "You did great," she whispered.

He gave her his signature grin as thanks.

A lawman stood up, drawing their attention. "Your Honor, I am Sisera Michaelson, and I represent the defense. I would like to crossexamine the witness."

The judge nodded. "Proceed."

Sisera turned to Seginus. "Sir, were you at one time a lawman?"

"Yes."

"Did you ever witness any instance where the lawmen twisted the law or held a fixed trial?"

"Yes."

"Please give an example."

"Certainly. John Lionelson, a minor under the age of eighteen, was summoned to court because he claimed to have seen the King and lived. I came as his defense lawman, aiming to cancel this tribunal before it began. Though his claim was impossible, it was not a legal matter to be discussed in court. He was also a minor, and, according to the law, minors were not to be prosecuted. For goodness's sake, the boy was fifteen!

"But the lawmen disregarded my reasoning, sound as it was, and held the trial anyway. It became clear that the only reason this bogus trial was being held was to eliminate John. The outcome had been determined from the beginning. The boy was declared guilty and sentenced, not to juvenile detention, but to execution."

The lawman picked up a large binder and leafed through it, finally putting his finger on a page. "Yes, that case was documented. It appears that the boy had also been causing trouble among his peers in classes, and his teachers had repeatedly brought it to our attention. He barely graduated with his class because of plummeting grades. It was clear that the boy was seeking attention, and when none was given, he became violent. One day John skipped class. That same day, another boy named Andrew argued with John about a random topic. The argument turned into a fight that was instigated by John, and Andrew came home with his face beaten until it was unrecognizable. The boy was a troublemaker from the start and had to be eliminated."

Seginus crossed his arms. "Do you know what the 'random topic' was?"

"That information was not given to us by the parents of either child."

"Mistake number one," Abi whispered.

"First of all, John's parents died in a fire when he was a baby. He had no parents. I was his legal guardian. Second of all, the 'random topic,' as you called it, of that argument was John's deceased parents. Andrew had said that John's father was a lazy drunk and his mom a whore. Naturally, John was incensed by that statement and did punch Andrew first. But the reason Andrew made that comment was because Andrew wanted John to fight with him but could not anger him with any of his previous comments."

"Did the boy tell you this information himself?"

"No, I watched this go on. You see, Andrew came to our house with the sole reason of instigating a fight."

"What was the boy doing at home on a school day?" Sisera was desperate now.

"He was at school. I gave him his schooling at home. He was an intelligent young man, far more than the lawmen gave him credit for. His testing scores were off the charts. I have them with me, if you would like to see them."

Trap number one is shut. You lose.

Shouts of anger and protest could be heard from the lawmen. The judge had to pound the gavel repeatedly for order.

The judge gave the lawmen an ominous look and said, "This witness is declared valid and exempt from any more questioning. The defense apparently does not have enough information to adequately question this witness any further."

Sisera, a deep scowl on his face, nodded and stepped down.

"This court is recessed until high sun."

Abi and Chris breathed a collective sigh of relief. The pressure was off if only for a few minutes.

The lawmen trickled out of the courtroom chamber and to their offices—probably to cook up some scheme for later. Chris stood up and walked over to review with Seginus what he would be saying next.

Abi wasn't sure what to do for a moment, but a quiet voice spoke to her heart. *Why don't you go outside for a bit? Some fresh air would do you good.*

Abi examined the idea for any flaws like she would a famous piece of art. Finding none, she stood up and walked to the courthouse door.

"Now where are you going?" a familiar voice whispered in her ear.

The Confrontation, Part Two

Abi warily looked over her shoulder. She smiled in relief at the sight of Nathan's grin. His merry blue eyes seemed to always be dancing with laughter, even now, during this tense confrontation.

"Just into town," she replied. Ever since Reilim's temptation and the King's subsquent assurances, Abi felt bolder and more self-assured. The promise that she had been chosen for greater things somehow infused new confidence in her, and she was able to push aside most of the lingering feelings of insecurity in every aspect of her life, including guys.

Nathan moved to walk beside her and opened the massive courthouse doors for her. "Can I come with?"

Abi pretended to think about it. "Well…"

He raised an eyebrow.

"I'm joking! Of course you can."

Nathan's grin had a slyness to it. "Great! Come on, I'll take you to a favorite place of mine."

Nathan watched Abi discreetly as he walked beside her. Her wide green eyes had wisps of blue that sparkled when she was excited, and endearing curls of dark hair had escaped from her ponytail and dangled beside her face. She clearly wasn't afraid to be who she was, and that in itself was appealing. Add that realness to her trim figure and bright-eyed wonder, and she was easily the most attractive girl he had ever met. *The guys in her world were all blind idiots. If she lived here…*

He jerked himself from that train of thought. He had known her for only a couple days, and, of course, they were from different worlds. She didn't seem like the type of girl who would only be good for a quick fling. Besides, Kes would kill him if he broke Abi's heart. He shouldn't get attached. All they had was a spark of…something…that they didn't have to explore.

But, in spite of all that, he couldn't resist the impulse to take her hand in his.

❧ ❧ ❧ ❧

Abi glanced at him when she felt him slip his hand around hers. His hand was warm and calloused and oddly comforting. She let herself enjoy his touch for a long moment then relaxed her fingers and slipped her hand from his. He was definitely cute, and he had helped Abi and her brother. But it would be unfair to him and herself to let him move past first base, only for her to go back to Earth and leave him here. There was no chance of a long-distance relationship there.

Then again, he could just want a summer romance. Then it would be all the more reason for her to distance herself, because he would just be using her. She wouldn't throw away her heart for a guy she probably wouldn't ever see again, but she would enjoy his company while she could. He was sweet, and that insightful comment in the woods was a point in his favor.

Nathan stared at her with a look she couldn't understand, then turned away. "Here we are," he said, not looking at her.

Abi looked around. They stood on a grassy knoll, and behind her, she could see the courthouse in the distance. "Why do you like it so much?"

"Come stand over here."

Abi moved closer to Nathan and was very aware of his nearness. *There's attraction here, all right.* She looked toward where he pointed. She gasped in awe.

Large snow-caped mountains loomed over the horizon. The sun reflected on their peaks, slivers of light shining in every direction. She followed one sunbeam with her eyes to a glittering meadow filled with brightly colored flowers and tall grass.

Filled with a sudden, wild abandon, she kicked off her shoes and ran barefoot down the hill and through the meadow. She pulled out her hair ribbon and let her hair flow loosely. She spun, reveling in the warm sunlight in the peace and comfort she felt. With an inexplicable assurance, she somehow knew that everything would work out. She knew the King had a plan, and this was his gift to her. As a cool breeze swept the meadow, her dress billowed around her, wrapping her close.

Relax, a cool breeze seemed to whisper as it swept through the field. *Stop trying to put everything in boxes and just…let go. Surrender, and find peace and joy.*

She lay down on the grass, putting her hands behind her head, and watched the fluffy, white clouds and bathed in sunshine.

After a few moments, Nathan came to sit beside her, gazing at her admiringly.

"I can understand why you are fond of this place," she said a little breathlessly. "It's so peaceful and lovely…" Abi looked toward the courthouse. "Even with such evil brewing only a few miles away." Her brow wrinkled in apprehension as she looked at the sun, now looming over her mockingly.

She sat up reluctantly, propping herself up on her elbows. "We should be getting back. It's almost high sun."

Nathan stood up, giving her his hand to help her up. "You're right. The lawmen probably won't be patient when they're the ones being accused."

She found her shoes and put them back on then reached to tie her hair back again. But Nathan touched her arm, and she looked at him curiously.

"Don't tie it. It looks nice like that," he said huskily, watching her long hair as it was tussled by the wind. He lifted a hand and tucked a strand behind her ear, slowly..

She raised an eyebrow but put the ribbon in her pocket.

They walked back toward the courthouse. Suddenly Abi noticed dark clouds gathering in the horizon, and she felt a drop of wetness on her head.

"Nathan?"

Nathan looked at the sky then at Abi. "Yeah, we'd better hurry. I think it's going to—"

All at once, raindrops showered on their heads. Abi squealed in panic, and Nathan made a run for the courthouse with Abi not far behind.

Right before they stepped inside, Nathan paused, and Abi almost ran into him from behind. "What is it?" she asked.

He turned around and studied her face carefully as if committing it to memory. Then he slowly held out his arms.

Abi looked at him appraisingly. If everything went according to plan, hopefully they would be able to go home soon after the trial. This may be the last time she ever spent time with him like this. All her logic warred with the voice that told her, *Let go.*

Tentatively, she stepped forward into his light embrace. A few moments of comfortable silence passed, and for a moment, when his arms tightened, she almost thought he would try to kiss her. But he simply let her go and opened the courthouse door.

By high sun, the court was in order, though no one could tell where the sun was. The heavy, dark clouds released showers of water, pounding on the courthouse roof. Chris took his place behind the prosecutor's bench, laying a few sheets of paper on the podium before him. The judge pounded on the gavel, and the chamber quieted.

"Prosecutor, you may present your next witness," the judge said, motioning to Chris.

"Your Honor, I would like to call forth Kesan Candial as my second witness. This man has also been an upstanding member of the community. As a merchant and businessman, he is known for his high standards and high quality of his work. As a neighbor and friend, he is compassionate, willing to listen, and generous, giving one-eighth of his earnings to the poor."

Another door behind the jury box opened, and out stepped Kes, who went to stand behind the middle pulpit.

Sisera stood up. "Your Honor, as the representative of the defense, I would like to cross examine the witness."

The judge nodded. "Proceed."

Sisera turned to Kes. "Kesan, have you ever been to a trial?"

"Yes, I have."

"Have you ever witnessed any abuse of power or unfairness by the lawmen in their dealings?"

"Yes, many times."

Sisera's face blushed with anger at Kes's slight. Attempting to control himself, he asked, his voice barely hiding his irritation, "Could you give us one instance?"

"Gladly. My best friend's sister, Charlotte Smithson, was accused of stealing a dress from my shop. I did not file the charge. Another man, whom I later found out was a no-account troublemaker who was angry at her because she rejected him as a suitor, supposedly saw her steal it while I was out on deliveries and told the lawmen.

"Since it was my shop, I came to the trial, though I knew nothing about what had happened. It soon became clear that the outcome had already been determined from the start. And even though the evidence Charlotte produced convinced me that she was innocent, no one consulted me, and the lawmen found her guilty. Her punishment? She had to bend over backward to pay me triple what the dress was worth. She was already living off her brother's income, not having a job of her own. If it had been up to me, I would have just let her off with a warning. But even though it was *my* store that she supposedly stole from, I could do nothing about her sentence. *Nothing!*" Kes was obviously enraged just talking about the injustice.

Sisera raised a hand. "That's enough, sir. Now," he leafed through the binder and pointed to a page, "the case that you speak of was, in fact, a hard decision. Of the jury, seven found her guilty and three not guilty—"

"Sir, that doesn't seem very close," Kes interrupted.

"Excuse me, but you interrupted me. I was saying that the *sentence* was a hard decision. But the jury agreed it would be easy for her to pay off the debt."

"*Easy*? Did you say *easy*? Charlotte was a single mother of triplets who became pregnant when she was eighteen because of a bad decision. She could not have a job because her hands were full from taking care of her kids. She had to take a nightshift job that lasted from midnight until dawn for two months to pay back what she owed. And even afterward, she slowly weakened because of the sleep she had denied herself for so long. She died the next year. So, sir, *easy* is not the word I would use to describe her punishment. And you didn't even know if she had done the crime!"

Abi sniffed and wiped the skin under her eyes, moved by Kes's impassioned speech. She wondered where the kids were now, and at that moment, her eyes met those of a young lady in the crowd. The girl smiled and wiped her eyes with a handkerchief then pointed to herself. Abi shouldn't have been able to see her mouth move with so much distance between them, but she saw the girl say, "I'm one of her daughters." Abi blinked then smiled through a torrent of tears.

Sisera was about to reply, but the judge interrupted, "That is enough, Kesan. You are exempt from further questioning because, and I think the jury will agree, the case you speak of is highly personal. The repercussions of punishment this lady received are not the affairs of the court."

Sisera, fuming, nodded and stepped down.

The judge turned to Chris. "You may bring forth your next witness."

Chris's eyes widened in shock, and he mentally slapped his head. But he had to respond. "Your Honor," he stuttered, "I only have two witnesses."

Abi could see Faln's lips slowly curve into an evil smirk.

The judge looked at Chris sternly. "By law, you must have at least three witnesses before you can present your case to the court."

Faln shot out of his seat, gleeful at this new opportunity. "Your Honor, this case is not valid without three witnesses. I suggest we quickly and quietly close this indictment before further wasting the court's time—"

Suddenly the courthouse door flew open with a loud bang, and all heads turned to see the source of this interruption.

Weana stood framed in the large doorway, her small nine-year old body shivering from the cold, her clothes soaking wet from the heavy rain outside and dripping on the dignified hardwood floor, but with a determined look on her face.

"I've come," she said loudly. "To be the final witness. To right the wrongs the lawmen have committed. And to set our town free of its demons."

The Final Witness

Faln had immediately sat down when the door opened, though not of his own will. It was as though invisible hands pushed him down. But at the sight of the girl, he became uncontrollably enraged. His fury consumed him, finally eclipsing his last tiny shred of decency he had kept intact after all those years of serving evil.

He shot out of his seat again. "The girl is too young! She cannot be a witness!"

The judge, meanwhile, had already thought of that and was flipping through a big binder. Finally looking up after a few moments, he replied, "There is no age limit to be a witness."

Abi swore she saw smoke come out of Faln's eyes. "Chris?" She tugged on her brother's sleeve as he was about to walk up to the platform to introduce Weana to the court. "Be careful. Faln isn't human." She shuddered.

Chris gave her his signature grin, though a little weakly, she noticed. So he, too, saw the danger they were in. But he composed himself quickly and walked toward the middle podium where Weana would stand.

"Your Honor, I would like to present Weana Candial. She is the daughter and only heir of Kes Candial."

Weana calmly walked toward the platform where the judge and jury sat. She curtsied masterfully to the judge then to the jury and slowly walked to the middle podium.

"Your Honor?" Faln stood up with his arms rigid at his sides and his hands clenched into fists. Abi braced herself for a tirade on why Weana could not be a witness, and it seemed the judge did, too.

But he surprised them. "I am Faln Cyrs, and I represent the defense. I would like to cross examine the witness."

Abi gasped in new horror. *Faln is going to try to embarrass Weana and annul her account as witness!*

Weana sat down on the couch behind the witness' podium, which was a move none of the other witnesses had dared to do. She appeared relaxed, leaning her head back against the now-soaked cushion. She looked indifferently up at Faln's smoldering eyes.

This seemed to make him all the more angry, but he held his irritation in check. "Have you ever been to a trial or lawsuit before with your parents?"

"Yes. My parents believed in exposing me to the worst to make me better."

Faln's face blushed with anger at Weana's implied insult. "Have you ever seen any unfairness or distortion of the law?"

"Oh, yes. In fact, I am proof of such. You, Faln, should know that. After all, you presided over it with great glee, if I recall correctly."

Chris sat up in his chair, curious at what else Faln had done. Abi, already half knowing, still listened closely as Weana recounted her interrogation and Faln's threat on her father's life unless she agreed to be his spy. She remembered it all down to the last detail of the shadow barrier and how it had knocked Kes unconscious when he tried to help her.

"How do we know this isn't just a childish fantasy of yours?"

Weana stood up. "Because of what you did afterward." She pulled up her robe's sleeve to reveal a small jagged circle on her shoulder that looked like it was burned into her flesh.

Abi and Chris gasped. "The mark of the spirits," they said in unison, remembering Micah's brand.

All in the crowd recoiled involuntarily, apparently already knowing what that sign represented.

The judge stood in the deathly silence that followed Weana's revelation. "The jury will make their decision in a few moments."

All eyes were wide with anticipation as they waited for the jury's verdict, and Abi and Chris sat forward in their seats.

The jury seemed to be arguing among themselves, and a few of the men even stood up, shaking their fists at the others. Abi saw the visible struggle in their faces as they decided whether or not to go against everything they had been taught. Finally, one man stood up, raising his hands for the rest of the jury to be seated, and spoke a few words. Slowly, the jury nodded, though some, including the irate men who had stood before, seemed surly in their agreement.

The man turned to face the judge. "The jury has come to a decision. The court finds the lawmen… guilty."

There were no shouts of victory, no rejoicing at the thought of justice. The lawmen were men just like them who had been led astray and corrupted by power and greed. They had sold their souls and gotten nothing but evil in return.

Suddenly the chamber filled with a mighty wind, and dark smoke rose up from where the lawmen sat. It seemed to wander around the chamber before a flash of golden-white light blinded the eyes of everyone. When it faded, the smoke was gone. And, Chris soon realized, so was Faln.

For a few moments, the courthouse was eerily silent. No one was sure what to do next.

But the judge watched them all with a curious smile on his face. Then he spoke. "I believe Chris has one last secret to reveal."

Chris stood up, though a little shakily. "The Stranger didn't die from a heart attack." Murmurs swept through the crowd at the mention of the Stranger. "He was killed by the lawmen."

An unnatural quiet descended as the people absorbed this new information. But it wasn't very hard to comprehend, and after a few minutes, someone in the crowd shouted, "The government is corrupt! Let us rule ourselves!"

"Yes!" others echoed. "Follow our own laws!"

"The people know the best justice for their own!"

The mob stood as one and rushed out of the courthouse in throngs, proclaiming in the streets, "Power to the people! Power to the people!"

"None shall rule us, not the lawmen, nor the King and his laws! We shall determine what's right and wrong!"

When Abi heard that last comment, she shot up out of her seat. "No! No! That isn't what you're supposed to do at all!" But her voice was drowned out by the crowd.

She looked pleadingly at the Judge as the courthouse doors closed. "Tell them, sir. Tell them they're wrong. That's not what the King wanted them to do with their freedom."

The Judge sadly shook His head. "Unfortunately, little one, I knew they would do it. With great victory comes great pride."

"But what will happen to everyone in Meynch now?"

The Judge looked at the small group intently. Chris had stood and laid a hand on Abi's shoulder, and Nathan had come to stand behind her. Kes put a hand on Nathan's head, and Marla leaned against her husband's ready arm, holding Weana's cold, wet body close to her. Jonathan and Aaren stood slightly away from the group. All listened closely for the answer. "Meynch will be once more plunged in darkness, but of a different kind. This darkness comes from the blind self-imposed rule of a fallible people. And soon light will once again be forgotten."

At the judge's words, golden-white light consumed the chamber. All fell on their knees and hid their eyes from the burning radiance.

As quickly as it had come, it disappeared, and Abi saw multicolored spots in her vision for a few moments. But when her eyes cleared, she gasped.

The courthouse doors had been replaced by the gate through which they had come to Meynch!

Moments later, she exclaimed, "It's the gate!"

At the curious stares, Abi attempted to explain, with help from Chris, how they had gotten to Meynch. But soon she gave up and turned to the judge. "Can we go now? We're done here, right?"

The judge smiled strangely. "For now," he replied.

Abi inhaled deeply and looked around at all the friends and family she would be leaving behind. She hugged Kes. "Good-bye, Uncle Kes."

"Take care, lass." Kes, without embarrassment, squeezed her gently.

Marla wiped away a few tears as Abi embraced her. "Good-bye, Aunt Marla."

Weana threw her small, thin arms around Abi's neck and sobbed loudly. Abi hugged her tenderly and whispered, "It's okay, Weana. You did well today. I'll miss you. But you have to be brave and take care of your mom and dad."

Weana sniffed, wiping her nose with her sleeve, and nodded. Abi gently put her down. Abi turned to Nathan. "Well," she said uncomfortably. "Good-bye." She stuck out her hand for him to shake.

Instead, Nathan bowed deeply and kissed her knuckles. "Farewell, fair lady. May we meet again someday soon." His sparkling, blue eyes, usually mischievous, now were intense and deep.

Impulsively, Abi hugged him, then held the back of his neck and kissed him. His surprise quickly changed to enthusiam, but she broke away quickly, and wouldn't look at him again.

She embraced Jonathan and Aaren together, and they awkwardly patted her back.

She waited a few moments as Chris said his farewells. He tried to be manly and unemotional. He shook Kes's, Jonathan's, and Aaren's outstretched hands stonily.

But when Chris bent down to hug Weana, holding her close, she simply touched Chris's face then buried her face in his neck. He felt the moisture of her tears on his skin. He blinked and straightened, wiping something from his face.

Finally they both turned to the judge at a loss for words. As they stared into his eyes, they gasped.

For the eyes of the judge were the eyes of the King!

The King smiled kindly and stretched out his arms to them.

Abi ran into his open arms, and Chris slowly followed suit. The King held them close, an embrace of tenderness and yet one of restrained power. "I don't want to go," Abi said. "I mean, I do, but not yet. I didn't get to spend much time with you or any of my new family. How are we going to keep in contact with them?"

A shaky half-smile lit Chris' face. "Yeah, it's going to be kind of hard to drop by for a visit, much less have a family reuinon."

The King let go and smiled lovingly at them. "But you will have another chance to see them. And you won't be leaving me here, at least." In a strange gesture, He cupped his palms out to them.

Abi and Chris touched small scars shaped like jagged circles in His hands and looked at Him in awe. “You are…you are…” Chris stuttered.

“I Am.”

They gave one last loving look to all they had met in Meynch, then faced the gate.

Chris reached out his hand toward his sister. “Together this time?”

Abi held it tightly and nodded, and they walked hand in hand into the light.

Seconds before they went through, Abi thought she saw an inscription on the doorway. She quickly took a mental picture so that she could remember it later. She somehow knew it was important.

Then everything disappeared in a flood of golden white light.

Finally Home?

"Ow!" Abi and Chris tumbled onto the plateau.

Abi stood up quickly, letting go of her brother's hand and looking around the plateau. Chris was trying to stand up using Abi's hand, and when, unknowing, she let go, Chris lost his balance and fell backward. "Ouch, ow, ouch, ow, ouch!" he said as he hit the stairs one by one. Holding his head in his arms, he tried to shield himself from the tree branches that hit him as he rolled down the stairs.

Abi laughed and followed him.

Once he reached the bottom, he promptly got to his feet, shaking himself off and rubbing the bruises he had gotten. "Ouch! If there had been any more stairs, I think I would have needed to go to the hospital!"

Abi giggled harder. "Now you know how I felt when I came through the gate before..." She stopped and looked up at the plateau.

There was no gate!

Chris looked up as well and noticed the bareness of the plateau. "What...how...why...how does it keep disappearing like that? Was it all a dream? Are we about to wake up?"

Abi, wide eyed, shook her head. "If it was, I dreamt it, too. There was Kes and Marla and Nathan and..."

"...Dad!" They ran to the back door of their house and threw it open.

There was Scott Candial, who was dressed in his bathrobe and slippers and sitting at the kitchen table, innocently drinking a cup of coffee. "Good morning, children," he said calmly.

Abi and Chris looked at each other, startled. Then they started talking at once.

"Oh my gosh, Dad, the weirdest thing just happened…"

"There were these stairs in the backyard…"

"We went to this place called Meynch, and it was a different world!"

"You were there…"

"And we met your twin…"

"And this creepy judge tried to kill us…"

"Slow down, kids." They quieted. "Now, let me see if I understand. You went to Meynch. You saw me there. You met my twin. You saw the Stranger. You confronted the lawmen. You fulfilled the prophecy."

"Yeah!" Abi exclaimed. "But we didn't say all that. How did you know?"

"Yes," Mr. Candial continued, "it was real."

Abi and Chris gaped at him. "So it's true? We really went to another world?" Chris asked.

Mr. Candial nodded.

"The King said, when Reilim tried to…you know, that our adventure wasn't over, that this was just the first step," Abi said. "Does that mean we get to go back?"

Mr. Candial shrugged. "You never know. The King is always full of surprises."

Abi and Chris continued to gape at him. "By the way," Mr. Candial said, "it's only 8:45 in the morning. Your mother will probably wonder—"

"Why are you dressed and up this early? And what are you wearing?"

They all turned to see Mrs. Candial framed in the doorway, still in her pajamas and wiping the sleep from her eyes.

Abi and Chris began to talk at once. "We went to another world!"

"Dad has a twin!"

"We met a King!"

Before they could say any more, Mr. Candial slapped his hands over both their mouths. "Oh, honey, you know kids," he said hurriedly. "They have the wildest imaginations. They were just telling me about their dream last night."

"Mmph!" Abi and Chris protested under their father's heavy hands.

"Well, okay, then," Mrs. Candial said, staring curiously at her husband then at her children. "I'm going to go back to bed. Remember, Abi, you're still grounded."

Abi nodded.

Mrs. Candial looked at them strangely then turned away.

Once she had left, Mr. Candial lifted his hands. "What was that for, Dad?" Abi complained.

"You can never tell anyone, and I mean anyone, about what you have seen in Meynch." Mr. Candial's face was grave.

"What? Why?" Chris asked.

"Beside the fact that people would think you were insane, Meynch is a very different place from Earth. Much of the evil that is in our world has not come into Meynch yet. You have seen the results of one man stumbling into Meynch: the corruption of the lawmen. If you were to tell someone about Meynch, and, even inadverently, the information fell into the wrong hands, it would destroy Meynch. Everything you have seen and experienced must be kept secret between us."

"Even Mom?" Abi said softly.

Mr. Candial sighed. "As much as it pains me to say it, even from your mother. No one must know."

While Chris thought about this new information, Abi had one more question. "Dad, I saw an inscription on the gate when we were coming back. It said…um… 'For many are called, but few are chosen.' Do you think it means something?"

Mr. Candial lifted his head and stared at Abi and Chris, who squirmed under his intense gaze. They were disheveled from their journey through the gateway, but their eyes were bright with anticipation. "Kids, do you understand the gift you have been given?

"You, for better or for worse, have been chosen for great things. The King has chosen you to fulfill his prophecy to the people of Meynch. Now that your eyes have been opened, now that you have begun the adventure, there is no turning back. And your lives will never be the same."

Abi heard, echoed in her father's voice, the King's words to her, and marveled at what had been revealed to her.

Unknown to all of them, three shining phantoms placed their golden hands on Abi and Chris' shoulders as Mr. Candial spoke.

For a moment, the teens glowed brighter than the sun.